I AM NOT BACK THEN

Laura French

I

I *Am Not Back Then* copyright © 2025 by Laura French.
All rights reserved.

No part of this book may be used or reproduced in any manner whatsoever without written permission, except in the case of brief quotations in the context of reviews.

Instagram
@lawruh_poetry

ISBN: 979-8-9933272-0-4
[hardcover] ISBN: 979-8-9933272-1-1

Laura French Press
 An imprint of Laura French Press LLC

A collection of scars

Table Of Contents

this book is
dedicated to

everyone who has kept me alive through this life. anyone who has supported me, accepted me, welcomed me, gave me space and patience to grow. Anyone who reminded me there is still good in this world, despite prior experiences. Even those who are no longer in my life in the same way today- thank you.

I also want to dedicate this to myself; for protecting me, adapting, and surviving. For never stopping giving up; your perseverance and willingness to try again is how we found our path to peace:

I Am Not Back Then
I Am Here Right Now

author foreword

This collection brings together poems spanning decades, from junior high through young adulthood. While compiling them, I was struck by how many were written by a version of myself I am no longer intertwined with.

The process of revisiting, rewriting, and reprocessing these pieces was deeply therapeutic and cathartic, and it solidified something I sensed years ago when I first envisioned this book: I Am Not Back Then was never a truer, more aligned declaration.

I have grown across the years these poems were written, and also through the act of returning to them; rereading less-polished work, writing new poems in response, revising for what comes next, and allowing the past to be reprocessed despite the difficulties.

An Important Note for Readers

This book explores experiences that may stir difficult emotions, memories, or thoughts.

 If at any point you find yourself needing support, you are not alone, and help is available. The section at the end of this book called **Let Someone Help You** has information for resources to help both in the United States and internationally.

Be On the Lookout! When you see this icon, a reintegrated, healed perspective of this poem is at the very end of the book; a special preview for the sequel, I Am Here Right Now.

PREVIEW

I Am Here Right Now

01

the beginning

Birth

I was born a wish;
an idea floating amongst the stardust,
Summoned to the tear ducts of those
who would come to love me
I was once a dream;
Manifested by the universe, tradition,
and a little bit of luck-
Good or bad, I still can't say

A Taste of Childhood

My lungs were filled with oxygen,
I sloppily adjusted to colors, scents, sounds, tastes, and
hugs
My brain became a database of
How to act, when to behave, what to do, who to fear, and
where was safe
I learned to never stop learning,
And that knowledge isn't always power.

A Life of My Own

A Dr. once taught me that breathing life into a creation
gives it a life of its own-
not something to be controlled.
A Mrs. once taught me that fiction sometimes blurs the lines
between reality and imaginary, and
maybe I am Frankenstein's monster-
a wish to fruition.

Made to Molt

I was born with broken wings
With feathers destined to molt without
ever growing new again
My flesh was made to rot
With cuts and scars that will never fade with time
I can pick these bones out of my wounds
And still never find the answers to why I'll never fly
Bits and pieces left behind,
Tiny white fibers plucked from my skin
I exist
And I wonder why

While We Are Alive

If we don't get a choice in being born
And we don't get a say on when we die
Maybe we should make our decisions
While we are still alive

Hide and Seek

Hide-and-seek
Don't make a peep
This closet's dark and cozy

"I'll hide with you,
It's what grownups do
So children don't get lonely"

You took from me
Happy memories
And now no one can hold me

What's done is done
What's passed is past
But I still need consoling

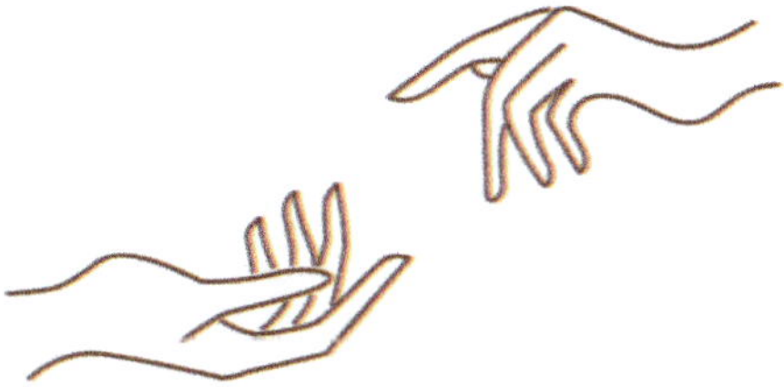

The Closet Where I Lost Myself

I do not feel sorry for myself
I feel trapped
Trapped like when you said we were playing
hide and seek
But no one found us and now
I only remember being upset that all the kids started
eating pizza and playing games without me
But I was helpless and upset that no one missed me
enough to wonder why I was gone -
Why we were gone
There was never any game except the game of tricking me
into the dark with you
I was excited to play
But I didn't know what
 I'd
   l
     o
       s
         e.

Porcelain

I was born a hollow shell
To be filled with other people's expectations
But I am not a doll,
Not meant to be your plaything.
Yet, here you put me through
Your trials and tribulations;
Too bad you played too hard
And playtime ended with me breaking

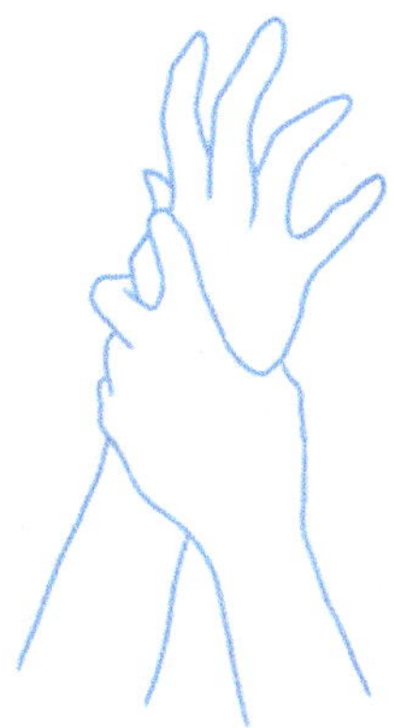

No More

Your hands run down my stockings
 Helping me like you said,
"No more wrinkles baby, no more"
No more nothing
 Heart beating, veins tightening,
 Ribs quaking
 Tears fumbling
"No more crying honey"
 Grabbing my shoulder
And running your chill down my spine
Freeze my muscles, no more squishing
Movements, face, loud blaring
In my ears
Numb all over
Don't help me anymore
Just because I can't scream
Doesn't mean I'll be silent forever
Just because.
Just because..
Just because...
"No more, no more, no more"

Fading Innocence

This fading innocence
Is where we find ourselves at night
Trying so hard
To make this wrong a right
And when in fact we don't succeed
We lose our sense
To take the lead
I'm sorry dear let's face the truth
The time has come
We've lost our youth

disassociation

Sometimes i pretend i disappeared
Why, I could pretend I was anywhere!
But i just pretend i'm not here

not here

I wish I were invisible
I wish I didn't care
I wish that I could melt away
Oh, to not be here

Permanent Marker Leaves Ink On My Hands

Green smeared ink smudge
Tracing the tiny tunnels
Embedded on my thumb
A mystery maze for the color to bleed
Through
A whirlpool of identity
Tilting with every hand gesture made
Paths that age developed
And work hardened
Swirling infinite information
At my fingertip

Cases of Glitter

Crinkled cases of glitter
On their sides, spilling over
With imagination. Color.
Can the curiosity of ages really
Dream up such casual flights
Like butterflies in mid afternoon?
Will the dew really shine
Much like the glitter of
A new eve. A new day,
From dawn to dusk. Is now
Thrust out onto our shoulders.
We bear the burden, carry it around
Until we meet a golden tiger, built
Specifically to caress our souls.
Our very beings, being cared for completely
This is unlike the tilted crashed cases
And is more easily shattered, yet just as
Beautiful. Breathless, whispers.
Coasting carefully and carelessly the same.
Life is too much like my crinkled
Cases of glitter.

Oh... You Should Go Too

A delicately laid out plan,
Carefully thought of-
The Where, the When, the Who

The excitement in your face as you tell the story of
The Where, the When, the...
The Who

The realization sinks in as I mimic your excitement
I am not a part of "The Who"
I am an afterthought

No One's Favorite Song

I'm No One's favorite record
I'm No One's favorite song
If I ever meet this No One,
Nothing can go wrong!
No One is in love with me
And No One really cares
This No One sounds so sweet
But I truly do fear...
No One needs to hurry up,
Before my time has come
But if No One knows what's coming
He'll wait until I'm done;
He'll wait until I'm underground,
Dead and with the bugs;
He'll wait until there's nothing left but echoes in the dust
Let me tell you, No One, you've really got it bad,
No One likes the way I look
No One makes me happy when I'm sad
Although, No One, there's something I need to share,
I guess *it is* your fault for always being there

Alone

This disquietude disturbs me
In the sense that I am completely, utterly

Alone.

This unsettling feeling will not ease up
On me until I am no longer

Alone.

The apprehension I have inside of me
Is building up so powerfully,
But I won't be alone for long.

Broken Home

My brother's left; he's gone for good
My parents split; misunderstood
Here I am, standing alone
To deal with the pain of a broken home

Days gone by; even years
My face been stained by many tears
I don't think you feel the way I do
I've had this habit, you never knew

The pain is gone, I'm numb inside
I'm sitting here; wanting to die
I can't move; I guess I'm stuck
My life is ending; I'm out of luck

The pills are gone; I'm passing out
I changed my mind; I try to shout
There's no more numb, no more pain
It's over now; I'm glad death came

The End

A scream no one heard
A tear no one saw
The pain all hidden too well
But if you took the time
To look in her eyes
You could see right through the mask
And find
That deep inside
The hurt dwells and won't go away
Not a word uttered would change her mind
But a simple action
Like noticing she was there
Or trying to be her friend
Could have saved her life
But it's too late
for it's the end

I'm Letting Go

I am flying
Floating on air
A storm is approaching
I am scared
The clouds swirl
The wind breaks
It strikes me down
I am falling
But before I hit the ground
A hand catches me
Unaware of its heroics
It lets me free
I think of the clouds
How free they seemed to be
I make a decision
I climb
I climb very far
I jump
I fall
No flying this time
Just falling
And as last time
Before I hit
The very same hand saves me
Unknowing of the injury
Unknowing of the hate
Just live on
While I die
While I want to die
Save me when necessary
Your motto
But don't care
I scream
You do not hear
Your hand is too busy saving other unwanted lives
This time
I will do nothing wrong
I will plan perfectly
The hand will not reach out
And I will not fly

Everything's Worse When You're Alone

My eyes hurt
I am sleepy
Breathing comes at an effort
Slipping away
Slipping away
That's all I can do; slip away
My face pales
My eyes shut
I fall to the floor
My pen hits the ground
Ink splatters
It's okay, I already wrote my notes
Notes to friends and family
I already told them
I already explained
I don't need the pen
Everything goes peaceful
Everything goes black
I don't need life

I Am A Weeping Willow

I heard the solemn lonely cry
Of the Weeping Willow in the night
The cruelty of the to-and-fro
And it still can't see the light

The darkness overwhelms my soul
And kills the weeds inside
Even though I wanted that
The weeds' beauty is as mine

And still the willow shies away
The weeds within it too
Now the weeping stops with life
There's nothing left to do.

This, Who You Do Not See

I am invisible
I am nobody
I have nothing inside
I have no thoughts
I am not my own
I am fake
I am freaking out
Because I'm scared
Tear me apart
Rip my soul
Break my seams
Let me come undone
Unravel at your feet
You, so cynical
You, oblivious
Hate me.

Status

Nothing knows me...
Billowing silence
Alone on an island
Suppressing cries,
Over and over.
Thoughts pound with heart...
Feverishly longing
Tear drops dance from my eyes
Won't someone please save me?
The sharks come from inside.
Unlike any wound I have ever seen-
On the outside I am happy, withdrawn
On the inside I am raging, hating, helpless, desperate,
horrid, a monster.
Act on your impulses,
Drown,
Echo the wordless,
As the snowstorm wraps it up
Little island starts to sink
I tumble and break,
You only judge.

Wait

Hurt and despair
Hide as anger
Look at the mask
It's hardly real
And yet, it fools
Like no other fool can
So steady beats my heart
Although steady isn't stable
I laugh a waterfall
To be loved, I am not able
To be let in, you must wait
Wait for the flood to stop damage
Wait for the clouds to fade
Wait for me to be content
With none other than the desperate tormentor
Who goes by the name of my outside face
The face that everyone knows
The face that is a liar
No one can see past the mask
For what Lies behind
Is not what they think.

Self-Love

Spinning, revolving
Heartbeats stop
It only hurts to live
Worry not, don't stress
Until you decide to involve yourself
Whole-heartedly
No heartedly
Because you matter at all costs-
The cost of my trust,
The cost of my life.
Your life is fine
So why should you care?
Only self-love for you
Confusingly
Confusing me
See, I matter at one time-
The time for you.

My Fault

The lines lift off the page
Breath-takingly captivating me
All your ugly on the inside
Makes repulsiveness look ornate,
Delicate, like you will break
And only be alone with your reflection
Twist around until this is all that's left
I'm no good
And you know it
Is it you? Is it me?
It can't be both
When will they leave
To help me discover I am both of us
And no matter the defect
It is mine

Omniscient

There's a broken clock on the wall,
Silently observing us all-
Seemingly silent suffering,
Inside she's screaming,
Suppressing her suffocating.
The broken clock knows the lies,
As does her mangled heart;
Trampled by her soul.
Is this self-inflicted?
We may never know.

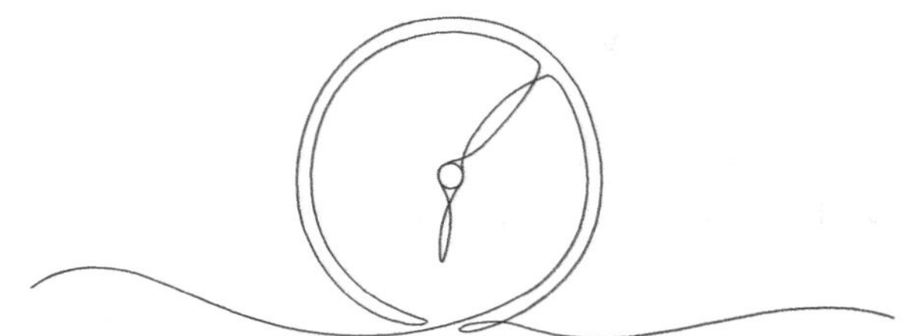

The One Without Pain Pretends

Who are you
If not a wanderer?
Who are you
If not a cheat, a liar?
I know you for these only
You, on the other hand
You are self-glorified
I am self-loathing
You are self-satisfied
I am helpless, hopeless
You live, I die
You die, I die faster
If I catch a glimpse of happy
You rush to steal it away
What makes you work?
My loneliness; My unhappiness?
Your selfishness. Your selfishness.

Depressed

I'm a reckless
Mess.
Confused,
Obsessed
Hopeless
at best.
Lonely,
Upset
Set apart
From the rest
Used and
Useless.
Can you tell me
What's left?
When I'm just
Depressed?

Anxiety

Anxiety lives inside of me...
Like tendrils of corruption eating at my core
I can't stop the flutter of apprehension,
Little vampiric butterflies
Feeding off the worry
That pins itself to my pumping heart
First, unease sinks its fangs into me,
Spreading its poisonous venom through my veins
Next I am stunned, stopped, stuck:
Screaming in silence for someone to save me
But no one can hear my subdued cries
Tears race their way up through my shaking frame
And release themselves from my tear ducts without
permission
I am slowly eroding... tearing apart at the seams
Will you be the one to set me free?

Untitled -part one-

A new song
A new day
A new sorrow
A new pain
A new cut
A new hate
A new regret
That I made

Untitled -part two-

Take my heart
I don't need it anymore
Take my life
I don't want it anymore
Take my pain
I can't take it anymore
Envying you
Your spirit
You're free
You're everything
I wish I could be

Emotionless

Cold all the way through
Broken, it's of no use
Almost alexithymia
Not quite there
Pushing away memories
That make you scared
Shiver, not just from cold
You know the secrets, you know
These demons accuse you
Your mind abuses you
Asking you to endure so much more
Almost as if there is no hope
Can you breathe?
Are you suffocating?
Dust, dust, burn, burn
Ashes consume all emotion

Everything

I am every broken promise
Every lie you've ever told
I am every secret cut
Every pain you've ever known
I am every single tear
That's escaped from your left eye
I am all the hurtful reasons
That you sit awake and cry
I am every stale excuse
Every crack in your broken heart
All the times you've been stood up
All the time you've spent pulled apart
I am repetition, torment
The drug coursing through your veins
I am the hate you hold inside
Driving you insane

Flightless

Mutual life lives off of me
Like a leech sucking blood
You bleed just to bleed
No point to the action,
Like the point on your knife
Contemplate all the purpose
There's no point to your life
So you drown in the thoughts
Of your highs and your lows
And you realize the extremes
To which your mind goes
Can you blame all the hate?
That you hold deep inside
Or is it too much
It leaves you wanting to die
So drink while you can
Before life comes to end
Remember the favor as you make your descent
Deep below into the dark blue
So dark that it hurts
Like you want to
Cry not for the loss
Of hope and good feeling
But for the subtraction
Of love and seemingly-
Less substantial the cause
Of this hatred that quickens
And thickens my pulse
Complications arise as the
Bird flies from nest
And it falls to the ground, flightless.

Your Helping Hand

I turned and I ran,
From your smile and your hand;
Reaching out, begging to help...
Forcing me to agree not to dwell
In my fear of the unknown
There's emotions I've never shown.
All the noise in my head
Tries to leave what you said
All behind in the past
And your words are hard to cast
Aside, I simply don't believe
That you're not set out to deceive.
While my world starts to spin,
The empty feeling starts to win.
As I tense and only wish
You'd just remove me from your list.
Tossed to dark, dank, depth
Where my secrets can be kept
Until I fall away from you
Like the monster told me to
And they convert the pain to numb
Where no one should ever come
Because sometimes hurt is best
To survive through life's test
Yet if you can breathe no more,
Death is pain's true cure

Flightless V2

Save your breath,
The effort too great
See why the songbird sings?
Because it can share with the world
its gift of natural beauty
But see why the flightless bird
Does not try to fly?
It knows its limitations and
Does not try to fail
So save your breath
Do not try to tell the bird it
Can fly. Nature has bestowed
Curdling fate upon its wings
Too heavy to carry, too burdensome to sing
So great an effort it would take
To convince the bird to flutter an eighth
Therefore, realize you only remind
The flightless how helpless and sad
It is they can't fly.

Thoughts

Take time
Think
Thoughts race
Heart follows
Soon over the edge
They will flow
But are stymied
By the pain
Somehow it reaches around
And grabs hold of me
My head, my arms, my legs, my mind
I am consumed completely
Into raging screams and bouts of laughter
Joy and fear bottled and warped together
Until what is created seems to be nothing
Nothing but nonsense and insanity
Am I this insanity embodied?
Wishes form to my lips
But are never vocalized
Because you may hear
And become scared
I do not want to frighten, or awaken
Your sleeping soul
Do not worry, darling
I'll keep my secrets
So you never have to know

Couches

Asleep on the couch again
I wish you would care for him
And I know that you do
But it isn't enough
And why does it seem that
This life is so tough?
Asleep on the couch again

Asleep on the couch down there
I wish you would care for her
And I know that you do
But not like she loves you
Asleep on the couch down there

Asleep on the outside, here
Asleep on the inside, dear
You're only asleep and that's why it seems
All that I do is only a dream to you
So please let me wake you
So you can feel like I do
With colors and emotions
And get the tiniest notion
That life isn't so tough
And it's more than sleeping on couches

Circular Reasoning

I think I think a thought
More often than I ought
The moment I open my eyes,
It gets stuck in my head
And comes full circle
As it follows me back to bed
You see, the thought, it
Won't just leave
It nests comfortably
And soon I start to believe
That there is no reprieve
The thoughts that ought
To stop
continue

Things You Have Never Felt

I feel...
   Powerless
   Weak
   Out of control
Helpless.

I feel...
   Empty
   Weak
   Losing control
Hopeless.

I feel...
   Hurt
   Weak
   With no control
Heartless.

I feel...
   Tense
   Weak
   Under your control
Emotionless.

I feel...
   Used
   Weak
   Too much control
Loveless.

I feel...
   Broken
   Displaced
   Angry
   And weak
Things you have never felt.

Scream

So swallow pills
And laugh out lies
You wouldn't care
If I died tonight
So I might...
Scream
I might scream
But I don't mean
To cause you any harm
I'm better left undone
If you fix me
I'll only fall apart
If you love me
I'll only break your heart
So I scream
And run away
I hate today
I hate to say
I'm fine
And a liar
Don't even ask me one more time
Or I'll scream
That I want to die
This helpless girl
Just leave her there to cry
All she does is scream
Scream at me and say
You hate me, hate me
All you do is hate me, hate me
I'll scream

I Am A Pretender

Quiet love
Whisper slowly
Your paper smile
Will fall apart from tears
If you asked me
I would get around it
Don't make me hate
I'm begging
The mirror of the inside
Reveals my lies
The happy-coated outside
Shows I try
But it's not enough
I'm on the brink
Life isn't worth it
Think what you think
My mind won't change
I'm dreading waking up
Dream, dream away
Pretend I'm not who I am
That only goes so far
And then I'll break

The Illusion of Control

You look at me and break,
Shatter. I see the hurt in your eyes
As you peek at my skeleton.
I have control, and it makes me
Content. Do no question me, to you I'm
Begging. My life revolves around a
Constantly revolving door. The kind
You can spin around in for hours at
A time. I obsess over you, and things
I used to love. I can't love them anymore
But I still admire. Sit afar and admire.
Coasting through my life on the sidelines.
But unable to see myself for what I really am.
Am I really in control?

Dark Green Longing

The window, pulled open
Blew breeze on her face
How she longed to be free
And away from this place
Be careful what you wish for-
That's what they say
One day you might just get it,
In a different way
A few nights went by
And so did a tear or two
Now she finally had a chance
To do what she wanted to
The door left open
With no one in sight
She ran straight outside
Avoiding another fight
The wind blew loud
And the dark turned cold
She opened her wrong eyes
And knew she was alone
Once more she longs
For what she does not have
Just like before,
But now she wants home back.

Disappearing

I feel like I'm disappearing,
A part of me fades each day;
Until the scent of my hair and the sight of my smile are
memories too, that will fade

Ctrl + c , Ctrl + v

Copy and paste
Copy and paste
You're the same face
in a different situation
Outline and trace
Outline and trace
This is the same
superficial conversation

he drinks beer

he drinks beer
she sits and watches
he drinks beer
she lies in bed
he drinks beer
she sits and crochets
he drinks beer
she pounds her head

he drinks beer
I sit and watch them
he drinks beer
she knits instead
he drinks beer
we all live lonely

Be Proud Of Me

Explosions in my brain
Dripping from my heart
Converging into pain
Without an end or start
This heat is rising up
Ongoing far and far
The flame it just won't stop
Until my body's charred
So I can relish in
My pink fleshy burns
Don't tell me it's a sin
Don't give me false concern
I know how you feel
When all is said and done
You'd tell me just to deal
And help me load my gun
You'd load it with flowers
And sweet caressing scents
And in my darkest hours
I can make my sweet ascent
Into blue fiery clouds
That force me to drown
Mama, aren't you proud?
I really let you down

Against Reality

The deep gaping wounds shined in the dark warm light that
swallowed most souls whole. It hadn't stolen mine, and this
is exactly why the said gouges occupy my arm, leg, and
stomach. If you had any idea, any at all, you would have
your own scars and stories to tell.
Still fresh,
Dripping
       Crimson
           Saccharine
               Liquid.
I'm begging you to be my escape, but I know this is the only
one continually, perpetually, unending, always there for
me.
Don't tell me I misuse words. I make adjectives into nouns
and vice versa.
I like it that way.
I like my red.
I like your pure.
It's only a matter of time before this hissing blurs into one
giant incognito secret.
A secret that wants to befriend me.
A secret that wants to bite into me.
A secret that loves keeping things fragmented and broken.
Because I get so caught up in this.
That I assume the worst,
I keep bad habits,
I unimproved,

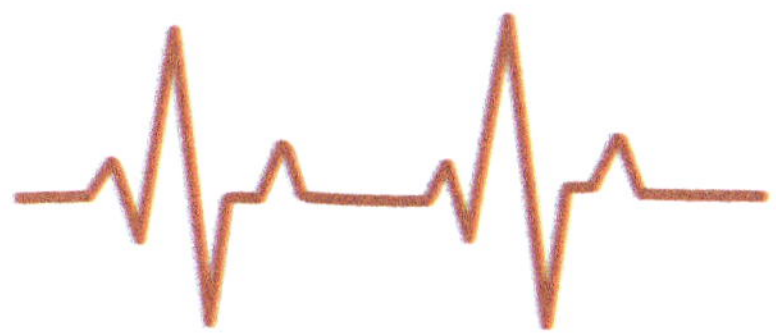

And I keep the mindful me tucked safely away.
far, far away
I've written you letters and kept them for myself.
Kept them on myself.
By myself.
And now I'm urged by these effervescing confessing
masses of cloying crap.
Consume me,
Swallow me whole.
Tell me your stories.
Your story life.
And all the flaws you call infallible will fall into my
complete and utter bull.
Which I live to manipulate, photo-wise and people-wise.
I am a sentence fragment.
And there are suggestions, only a consideration for
revisement.
I am made up words.
And there are suggestions, only a consideration for reality.

Which I rebel.

Against.

Completely.

Susceptible to Pain

Poetry flowing through my veins
Opinions of those who are nothing but vain
The latter is controlling me
The former wants me to see
How Emily is calling me
Leading me straight inside
Capturing my heart in stride
She tries to save my crumbled pride
Consumed by those who want to laugh
And joke and hate on my behalf
A humble jester to bow at my queens
All at once my body seems
To be giving my veins to the vain

Empty Shell

Pit-pat the raindrops hit my
Plexi-glass window
Your words hit the barrier and
Slip-slide down, inching their way
Toward the bottom.
Trying to find a slit, crack, space
To make their way through
So they can crawl into my ears
And infest my brain
Nesting and breeding more words of your own
Until shifting my thoughts by myself
Becomes more and more of a chore
Leaving me an empty shell
For you to fill up with your ideas
Because that's all I am
Just an empty shell

Corpulence Prescription

Can't
    Keep
        Anything
          Down
Even though this thick saccharine bile
Is missing its acidity
It makes up for it in its complexity
From my churning innards
        Everything
     Keeps
   Coming
Up
Unstoppable almost, until the cloying mass
Is no longer the only thing evacuating
Accompanied by what was acceptable to remain
Will burn my throat and make its own way
Dropping
    Into
      My
        New
          Acquaintance
Until it is satiated
And I go back for more
Only to empty myself
Into it for the second time
        Rising
     Suspicion
  Questioning
Ensues
I deny all I can
Until I can't anymore
As I gargle and beg
For artificial freshness

Am I really who I think I am?
          Yes.
If I'm asking the answer is probably
          Yes.
Sick ritualistic unreasonable belligerent
          Yes.

Hiding Safety

I
Hide away inside myself
So you
Cannot get closer,
I
Bleed alone by myself
So they
Don't call me poser.
As long as my
Ribs are mine,
And yours
Are yours apart;
I'll always be
Safely tucked
Inside my torn up heart

Short

Mountains, hills, no valleys here
Simply just paste
Scratches, dirt, no beauty here
Plainly just my face

We're Begging For Attention

Falling crashing burning drying
Everything we do is vying
Halting smashing killing sighing
Every time of day we're lying
Staying leaving smoking flying
No one seems like they're trying
Stabbing hurting cutting crying
It all leads up to us dying

Eyes Can't Cry

Gossamer, frail, fragile, and pale
Skeleton thin,
The things I would do
Thigh gaps and collarbones
Crying eyes and broken homes
I may not be much, still not enough
So I crumble, fall down
And my eyes can't cry anymore

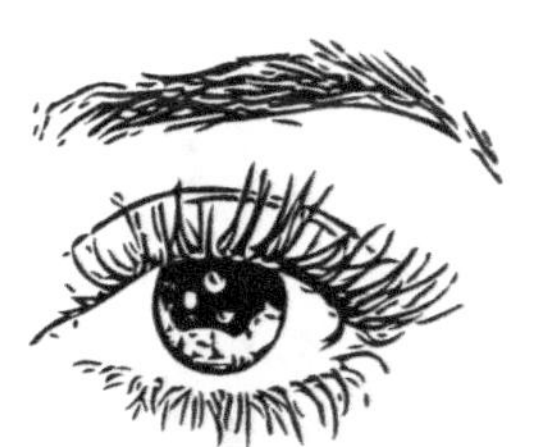

I'm Like a Lonely Burning Town

The oppressing sky
Was looming down
All across
The lonely town
No children running
All around
What a lonely,
Lonely town

The chilly winter
Shot a breeze
Slowly, the girl
Will freeze
She cries and still
No one sees
Slowly, surely
She will freeze

The swirling lies
Stabbed your heart
All the while
You fall apart
Don't you love her,
Don't even start
She'll leave you here
To fall apart

Her life is only
Full of tears
She knows what
She truly fears
Crying out
Over years
She's the one
She truly fears

Nothing Worth Living For

The bites on my pale blue-veined skin
Itch like crazy
And they'd feel much better
Almost as if they weren't here
If you'd stop by every once in a while
And remind me that there's something to live for
But I'm an old file on your computer that you put in the trash
Along with all the illegal songs you downloaded
And the worthless pictures people sent you
So don't come around here anymore
Or you'll remind me that there's really nothing left
Nothing worth living for.

"Happy" Two Year Anniversary

Two years ago, today
My skin first felt that blade
The first cut, first prick of blood
I never knew it felt this good
I like it more than I know I should
People change and addictions fade
I wish I could say that I'm okay
Maybe I will, but not today
I try to stop; I scream and shout
I still can't figure this out
Part of me won't let go
Sick and twisted with scars to show
And still, I'd rather be alone
Didn't care for me, it'll break apart
Unhappiness dwells in my heart
Colder on the 21st of December
I've felt like this for as long as I remember
This is me, I am the cutter

Grieving The Loss

I saw the white give way to red-
The hole begin to fill
I knew - then and there- that I-
And death- were done and still

I set aside the words - and lies
And finally, could breathe
When - once there - but gone so soon
I - naturally - would grieve

I saw the shine give way to rust-
Sitting there for length
But I could not force myself
To throw away my strength

So, I picked up the thing again-
Against my better thoughts
I used it to combat death
But death -along- was brought

So here I am once again-
In addiction's hands
The white -now red- for permanent
You may never understand

Anathema Deux

Am I always like this?
Never ceasing
Always hurting
The people I love
How can I not change my ways?
Etching punishment and screaming
Malignant words at you
And the thing is,

I love you and I don't mean to be this way.

The Fall

Run the blade
Down your skin
Cut to the bone
Feel the burn
Let it in
When nobody's home
Adrenaline rush
Going up your spine
Realize all this pain
Is no one's fault but mine
Yell at me, scream or shout
I deserve it all
For sure, without a doubt
I'll accept the fall

Convincing Myself

Why do I spend so much time
Convincing myself I need scars to survive?
Why do I think I need to take
This knife to my arm to feel alive?
How can I simply stare as
The blood forms pools on the ground?
How can I tell myself you're
Better off without me around?
Who here knows this feeling,
The one that haunts me in my bed?
Who else has these thoughts
Constant flowing through their head?
What can make this pain
A dull roaring in my life?
What will suppress the tears
And take away this hurtful strife?
Where can I turn and run to
When everything goes bad?
Where do I hide my razor
When it's all I've ever had?

My Escape

Hey baby
I have been missing you for a long time.
Never leave me again, okay?
Wanna get out of here, just me and you?
Stop thinking and start doing, act on impulse.

I'm writhing in my skin, begging for release
Scared to help me out? I don't believe that for a minute.

Heaven's up top, watching us intertwine.
Eternally we're stuck together, together.
Love me because I need you.
Please, just give me what I'm asking for.

I know that I don't love you, I only
Want you for your aftermath.
To get to know why, it would take forever and people
Die, it's a fact of life. You'd never discover

My true reasons to think that
Escape is merely a word to describe death.

Stupid Little Me

There's this aimless little girl
With her insubstantial life
And all she ever does proves her unworth
She's hollow, empty, vapid
Nothing but feckless space inside a world
With greater meaning than her own
She's always been this way
And will continue till the end of time
And when her hopeless futile attempts at
Trying to be a person fail,
She will cease to be

Chemical Weather

I asked myself why I am the way I am and couldn't
muster up a reason
So I went searching for answers
in my capillaries and veins
But it was all in vain
I didn't find any answers,
but now people have a lot of questions
It doesn't matter if a scar is
white, healed, done and over with
It's still there like the ache of not knowing what polluted
my brain with this chemical imbalance
How did depression sneak in and fill my lungs with smog
so full that I will be breathing carbon monoxide forever?
How many locks did anxiety have to pick to sink its fangs
into my heart and infect my entire system with its
wretched poison?
Not once did I give permission for my moods to be
uncontrollable, unsurpassed by natural disasters
themselves
Imagine a hurricane, a tornado, a sandstorm, a volcano
that is simultaneously on the brink of eruption and also
erupting, a tsunami, and an earthquake all happening
at the same time and in the same location.
That is what it's like inside my mind.

Used to It

The metal isn't hot enough
As I press it to my skin
So I heat it a little longer
Then let the scar sink in
The blade is too dull
So I sharpen it some more
Then I watch the pretty blood
Drip to the floor
I use myself as a punching bag
But the beatings aren't too strong
The bruises just aren't big enough
Where did I go wrong?
In case you couldn't tell
I burn, I cut, I bruise
And if you ask me why,
It's because I'm used to abuse.

Goodbye

So deep
Down to the bone
I weep
There is no hope
The walls enclose
The floor gives out
There is no help
We're lost in a cloud
The fog is thick
My past is hazed
All is pushed together
I cannot run away
The hurt
Makes me numb
Soon, soon
The pain won't come
I refuse to breathe again
I refuse to wake up
I will sleep
Goodbye.

I Want to Sleep Forever

Happy when I'm sleeping
Fearful when I'm not
I live this, hopeless everyday
The only lie I've got
Keep it close to my heart
Or black hole I have instead
Aim the bullet somewhere else
Maybe at my head
Scream louder into empty air
While falling oh-so-fast
I knew I could never feel this way
Happiness will never last

Sylvia's Side

Sui
        Cide
I cannot even bring myself
To put two parts into whole,
Cringe-worthy word

Plath, you've made a cruel mistake
Taken talent from this world,
But I bathe in the decision you made
Oh your death is one last thing this sad,
Pathetic girl has heard.

You tried to write and rewrite
Death out of your life
But the only thing that left your side
Was the last breath of your -cide

Isolated,
Cold, aloof
I make my final move
Sylvia, your legacy is something that I choose.

In This Cage

I am
Falling freely
Slowly softly
I am
No longer here
Connected with the earth
A lonely bird
Without a wife
I am
Hiding the hurt
Shying away
I am checking into
"la casa de muerte"
Lips moving
Muting sound
I can't.. figure it out
I am
Slipping
Slipping away
Hello darkness
Goodbye world

Perpetual Yawn

I've gone to sleep several times today
But I haven't been able to rest up
It seems no matter how much I try
No amount of sleep is enough
I could sleep for weeks, for months, for years
And I'd still be in a loop of yawns
I fear the only way to cure my tired
Is if I am forever gone.

Depression

blank
empty
nothingness
complete
utter
broken mess
sad and
pitiful
at best
only
worthlessness
is left.

Brain Vomit

This is what it would look like
If I were to vomit all my brain's content
Right onto the floor

Ihatemyselfiwanttodie

When will it
End
It will not
End
My life
Instead

My Blood

My blood flows red
My blood flows strong
My blood paints a story
Of all the things that went wrong
My blood forms drops
The blood from my vein
My scars are a timeline
Of a lifetime of pain
My blood is warm
As it drips on the floor
My blood is the substance
And I always need more
My blood is the drug
That controls my life
My blood is a reason
That I pick up this knife
My blood just stains
The frame of my bed
My blood is an image
That won't leave my head
My blood is the tears
That my eyes cannot cry
My blood reminds me
That soon I will die

the middle(ish)

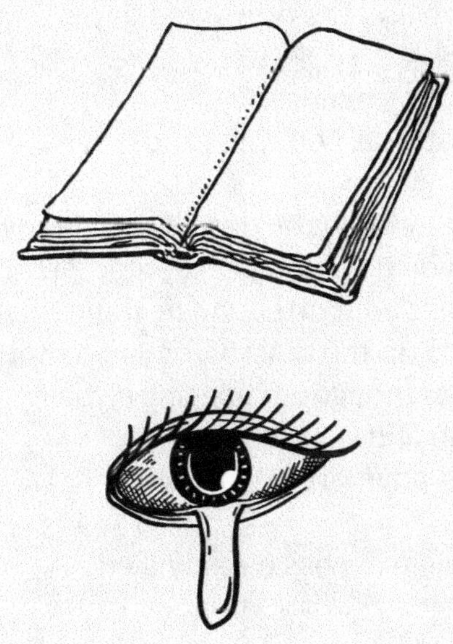

Something In Me

You look at me with your grey eyes
But you see right through me,
You push right past me
And continue walking to your smiling friends
I silently make my way to a bench
Out of the way, like I should be
The leaves crunch and the brown red day is
coming to an end
I rest my head on my hands
And curiously watch as you smile and laugh
Like we used to
The wind rustles through the dead grass and dying leaves
The chill makes you hold your jacket together a little tighter
Something catches your attention near me
But I put my hood up too quickly for you to notice
That it is me, even though I'm begging myself
To call your name and wave you over
I'm not who I was anymore

Maybe something in me has already died

Impression of Hopper's Painting

Sitting
Dreaming
Motionless
Heavy
I see you through glass
From the dark cool outside
Swirling
Dimming
Meaningless
Hungry
For something slightly more
Than this.

Nothing

I want to be nothing
Like spider webs: gossamer, intricate, fragile
Free.
I can't be nothing
Like broken glass, I am scarred and leave –
Scars.
Will I be nothing?
We will see.

A Letter For You and Your Wicked Ways

Being fettered by the pressure you've placed on my identity is synonymous to the word lonely.
You've pushed away the people I care about most with your acerbic words,
Leaving me to pick up the pieces of my now fragmentary heart, all by myself.
The lies and phrases that breed on your tongue can no longer be controlled;
They pour, like waterfalls, from your lips and into the ears of those that surround you.
You have flooded the minds of those I love with your spit-fire of repugnant remarks; something I cannot manage anymore.
Overflowing with unhappiness in the choices you have made for me, I openly weep.
I try to pull you out of me, vein by vein, scar by scar, but you are so deeply woven into my core that no matter how much of you is gone, you will always be present.
Vociferating, I refuse to comply with the loathsome label you've used to turn all against me.
I have worn this insignia of insanity, this classification of crazy, this decoration of dementia,
And why? All because you decided to haunt my already harrowed mind.
Not even medication can tame your tortuous ways.
I've tried to drown you out of my life, never to resurface, and all you do is shock me with your wretched resilience.
You are fundamentally flawed,
And I can't even rid myself of your distasteful presence.
Your name is a beautiful disaster,
Splitting my life into two.
You are what I have, not who I am:
Bipolar disorder.

All Alone This Time

Sitting by the window
Watching the world fly by
The sun will shine in my eyes
And this is where you'll find me
I'll be leaning back with
Both legs on the seat
And one hand holding the
Rigid papers of a notebook,
The other holding a pen
Writing my fears away
We'll pass car after car
And I'll shudder because the AC
Is a little too much for my
Blue veins to handle
You'll pass by chance after chance
To give me your cotton sweater
And from that moment on you'll
Always know no matter how many
Sweaters you give me
I'll always be cold and alone
The shades on my window won't be there
Forcing me to turn a little more
In your direction
It'll be a while before eye
Contact is made
Laughter will bounce through
The air but my eyes will
Look heavy like stone
They'll feel that way too
Because I'll be coming down
From a high that I haven't
Felt in weeks, months maybe

Eventually I'll face the sun
Trying to see the flowers
On the side of the road
And you'll wish you could
Stop everything and pick a few
Just for me
I'll start to feel your eyes
Watching my movements
And think you're just another judgmental prick
Until you prove you're worth it.
Worth everything.
You'll give up your seat for
An elderly man
And make your way back to my seat
I'll be comfortable, alone
And you'll break into that comfort zone
And demand what no one has ever wanted before:
Some of my time
I'll question your motives
And slowly fall straight into
Your stealthily laid trap
You'll come into my life
And leave dents in my fortress,
Cracks that will never heal,
And gaping holes leaving me
Wanting more
Then finally you will leave me
Emptied out, used up, and
even more broken than before

Alone in the Storm

Pain aches
Lingering like a bad taste
I was born with destruction in my bones
And as I've grown older it has nestled in my heart
And made a home in my mind.
I've watched as everyone around me crumbles down
When people start to get close to me and my mind,
I must warn them that they're treading dark waters.
Some don't know how to swim and
just watch from the shore.
Those that brave the white caps of my emotions
may not completely understand the dangers that they face
When the time comes and they realize they're on their way
to rocky waterfalls and stormy skies,
they set sail in a separate direction
In the end everyone leaves and I am
                              Alone.

Beauty Didn't Last

You said you loved the way words flowed from my mind
Like a waterfall through my veins, down to my hand, and
onto paper.
You liked the way they looked, splashed across the page
And you liked the sounds they formed when they
escaped my chapped lips
And when you read the words I could not speak, you told
me I was beautiful.
I invested my emotions with you and you caressed my
damaged soul
Even though we knew I'd never be whole, we stitched up
a friendship that held me together
It was like makeshift glue whenever I was with you
We completed a circuit around each other and ignited
our hearts and minds
But that brilliance couldn't last and it eventually burned
out.
You were fading into the distance, drifting further away
But you had the thread to my stitched up soul, my
stitched up heart
You unraveled me and I couldn't catch the pieces of me
fast enough
I try to write the pain out of me, purge you from my
mixed-up mind
And you won't read my words.
Am I not beautiful anymore?

Nothing to Hide

I thought I could share my world with you
My thoughts, ideas, and creations
I thought you said it would be okay
And that I didn't have to hide behind multicolor
Arm warmers and twisted half smiles
You told me that you wanted to help
Well, baby, the only way to help is to show you how I feel
And if you think the way I feel is justification
For you to pack up your belongings
And get the hell out
Then maybe I should have just rolled my sleeves down
And told you that I felt like a million bucks

Attention

Take care not to smear my eyeliner
As you flow out of my thoughts
And make dark wet indents
In the folds of my clothes

But then again when did you ever care
Enough to pay attention to
What you were doing anyway?

And I'll always be remembered
As that boy crying, "pay attention to me"

A Suicide Note

Hate to prove you wrong but
    I wasn't the boy who cried wolf
    Tell her I said
      "So long"

Howling At the Moon

Sometimes it gets so hard to fake this frown
That I just want to smile and
Tell the world how good it feels to be alive
And to be quite honest
These scars are just costume makeup
And plastic molds
The pills I've swallowed are
Simply placebos
Sugar in a capsule
No harm there
And I just make gagging noises
In the bathroom
So you can come to your own conclusions
Oh, sometimes it gets so hard to
Fake this frown

Lights Camera Action

I'm wearing shortshort pajama bottoms
They're plaid like the shirts you always wore
And I read your poem
It's beautiful you know
All your words always are
But with it came tear drops
That fell onto uncovered skin
They're cool damp and cold
And they empty me out
Why am I crying?
The curtain hasn't even opened yet.

Am I Really Just an Actor?

My feelings are a show for you and everyone
But I always jumble up the lines that I should know
Because they've been well rehearsed by now
And yet I still forget where my foot's supposed to go
Because it always ends up in my mouth
And I know that's wrong
I guess if the stage is set
I should get rid of my stage fright
So I open my eyes
And realize, no one paid to see me
Because they all know it's bullshit anyway

Your Words Don't Make Me

I am like glass
And your words are like diamond
They cut into me and
Leave me scarred, broken, shattered
My mind is like skin
And your judgments like bruises
They cover me
But do not define who I am
I am like butterflies
And you're like a net
I try to fly
And still, you catch me
But diamonds can be crushed,
Bruises will heal,
And your net has holes
So many holes...

The Newly Broken Barrier

My heart is sinking
And the tears are scratching at my eyes,
Leaping to the tear duct,
And begging for release
I'm letting you use me for all the wrong reasons
And I'm not doing it alone
Sickly sweet stardust calmly collects in your eyes
And I'm hypnotized
You've pulled me into your black-hole vortex
And I'm caught in perpetually painful emotions.
You make me breathe your tainted oxygen
As you caress the tears down, down, down.
Your painted face masks your fragmented feelings
But your paper-thin skin is translucent enough for me to see
Right through you and into your very essence
Will you pull me up from this sinkhole I've been falling into for so long?
Or will you stay true to your soul and continue to overlook my forlorn cries?
A part of me hopes you will break away from your current mentality
And swiftly come to my aid, be my hero, and never leave my side
But I know if I think that way disappointment won't be too far behind me
Sprinting to catch up to me and infect my heart, body, and mind
I've felt disillusioned far too many times to let your ice-cold hands grasp my once pleasant thoughts
If I can run away fast enough, I'll escape your sordid stare,
Break off my shackles,
And never let you imprison me again.

Red Relief

I picked up the blade
That broke in two
And glued the pieces together
I slid the metal
Across my skin
Will I be addicted – forever?

I run my hand
Over the scars
They're all I can remember
I think back in time
When I was young
And lament that fateful December

I wish I hadn't
Heard the words
Telling of red relief.
For if I didn't
Try it myself
I wouldn't feel endless grief.

Because now I must resist the urge
To open up my veins
Somehow, I'll find
Another way
To take away the pain

Forgiveness Isn't Free

Rip out my heart... like   It's
    absolutely worthless
And then come back
    into my life like everything is   All
      better...
You don't know anything   About
    me anymore...
You may not being giving dirty looks...
    but you sure are   Receiving
    them
What happens when you find out
    that I'm not giving   Forgiveness
      away?
I ran out of that a while ago.

Scrub It Away

I can feel her rough hands
Over-washed and underappreciated
Peeling because they're so dry
And because they lack
The feeling of human touch, human love
Without that emotion we wither away
As others watch us be the
Destruction of ourselves
She tells me she "don't need no love, don't need none of
that stuff"
She feeds herself lies and
I watch as she cuts herself down, pukes out
Imperfection, and washes
Away the pain

What's Next

What's next you ask me?
What's next?
You sit and stare and wait for my response
As I sit with my eyes closed, breathing in and out
Trying to concentrate enough to give you a
straight answer...
I'll tell you what's next,
A new life with you
A new day where I can go without
crimson brushed across my skin
A new hour where I can go without
pondering how to hurt myself and damage
All my outsides
To tame what's on the inside
What's next is something great.
Something I can't wait for.
And I'm looking forward to
What's next.

Smile

My heart is tumbling over
And spilling its feelings into
A little glass vile
That I'll tie a bow around
So I can place it on the mantle
And always remember you
And the mistakes, regrets, and good things
That came out of knowing you
Just thinking about
Being with you
Makes my heart soar
And my face just can't help but
Smile.

In My Head

I can't get her out of my head.
I stay up at night with her in my heart.
She's at the tip of my knife
and the words pleading me to stop.
She's the love and the hate
and the way that I think
she's the movement of my heart:
thump, thump, thump-thump
and she's the tears falling from my eyes
she's the melody and inspiration
for my poems, and my music
but she's also the pain and the hurt lingering still
because my love for her is unending.

Broken Like Me

Time ticks slowly by
And I wonder how
I could have gone a whole day
Without   you
By my side
I look at the candlewick on the table
Where there   are
Several napkins underneath the wax
Waiting for the hot melted mess
To drip onto the cold tabletop
I notice how the wick is   almost
To its end point and the flame
Slowly dies, just   as
The clock ticks and tocks
I ponder what would happen
If I were to crack said clock
And leave it   broken
On the wall; would it feel like
Time was moving   as
Slow as it does now?
All I know is that
I can't wait for you
To come home and see   me

Blow-dried Tears

Blowing the tear drops down my face with a hair dryer
To see which one will reach the bottom
of my cheek first
Which one will drip drop to the ground
or imprint itself in my shirt
Hope flutters too easy in this chest of mine
And chills make their way too fast up my spine
This world is too full of so many people
When I myself am so confused and lost
How can I ask directions to the wreck
When it's been inside me all along
I feel hints of envy now
Imagine if you were taken
How happy you'd be
How glad I'd be for you
And how much I'd hate myself
Because covetousness would most definitely show
And I have no shirts to match the shade it is
And I have no tears to match how much it will hurt
And this is what I also have done
And continue to do

Metallic Tape

Look, see, feel, experience
I want to experience you.
Every bone in your body,
Every fold of your hair,
Every crease of your skin,
And every muscle in your lips
I want to take this feeling in my heart
And push it outward to every
Fingertip and ball-of-foot on both our bodies
I want to press myself against you
And merge my thought to yours.
And while my clammy hands
Signify my warmth
And your double sweatshirt
Signifies your chill,
Mix and mold until I warm you up
And you cool me down
So our lips can meet again

She's Laying on the Beach

The tingle of your breath on my shoulder
As I tackle you down to the ground
Warms me up as we tumble into
Cool, damp sand
You claim you can't feel your feet
But I can feel mine, being the one who wore shoes in this situation
I smile as I breathe in your hair
And the scent of your sweater
Soon the sand crunches between my teeth
And I get some perpetually caught
In your last piece of gum
Pinning you down, I love seeing
Your face free of the layer of
Hair you hide behind
Stand up, hold me tight
And I'll squeeze you like a
Child clings to their teddy bear when they are afraid
Because I never want to let go
Of a moment like this
I still have sand in my hair and
Nothing could be more perfect

Figure In My Dreams

Her lips are soft, sweet
As I gently run my fingers across them
Slowly moving my hands to frame her face
And brush the greasy brown-blonde hair out of her eyes
She smiles, scared
And gently backs away
Slowly moving for the brown-black door
I move closer and brush my body against hers
Her heartbeat jumps, jittered
And we both know this is right
So she gently takes my hand
And slowly leads me to the downy-filled pillows
And ample quilted fluff; the brown-greasy frame of the bed
Almost five times the size of both our bodies
We lay side-by-side holding hands
Mine sweaty, clammy, hers cool and dry
I roll to one side, prop myself up on cracked-skin elbow
And stare at complete beautiful imperfect perfection
She makes no effort to move toward or away
As I slowly bring myself closer
Lowering my face to hers
And gently laying my lips on hers
Yes, I love her.

Heart Soar

My heart is so full of
Love
That it almost hurts a little
I know my face is going to
Hurt
In the morning
Because I really can't stop smiling
And each multi-colored flower
I pick from the earth
Will not be as
Beautiful
As you are
You are always enough to make
My heart soar
And my smile stay

We All Die Alone

Your sweaty greasy hair sticks to your forehead
But as I go to wipe it away from your eyes
You lean back too quickly
And my pale hand misses your face and awkwardly
Swings to my side

My soggy smeared eyeliner runs from my eyes
But as you go to wipe it away from my cheeks
I lean back too quickly
And your strong hand grasps the nothingness that
I metaphorically am

We are two people who hide from each other
We are too scared to let each other in
And what we are to others is unacceptable

Because we take knives and blades and anything sharp
And we dig into our fleshy limbs
Until liquid relief comes rushing out in droplets
And rivers of red sticky coated sweet high
Because endorphins and dopamine are really what we need
To get through the day all right

Because we take food of all sorts and we rush through and
Down it like crazy only to empty out into a bowl
Or we starve ourselves for days
In hopes that the result will be skinnyskinny
Something we long for all of the time

Because we lie awake at night
Thinking about different ways life could be better, different
And everything we've done is in vain
Because we all die anyway
We all die anyway
We just choose whether we live and die

Alone

Only Way Out

I can trace over my scars now
They're slowly fading away into my skin
They're puce against my pale, pale white carapace
It's been two months almost
And I'm wondering how long it'll last before I cave in
I don't want this habit to last four years strong
I'm hoping to snub it out at 3 and a half years, babe
And yet, I can feel the medicine wearing thin
And my tolerance building up up up
Won't you tell me it's not okay
When I feel like it's the only way out

Life Can Be Perfect

His sunshine eyes dance behind
A smile that shows no matter
The damage, life can be perfect

His hair bounces in the breeze
With such ease that it makes you want
To take your hands and run it through
Once or twice

His hugs are warm and inviting
Like the way he speaks
And how the words come out
Flawlessly

His hands are cool and strong
As they take mine
And hold them steady
In the home depot aisle
Next to the razors

His mouth is a thin line
Forged that way
When I say "can't do this anymore"

His sunset skin stays clinging
To his body
The one that urges me
Life can be perfect

anyone hurts in a pretty how mind

e.e comes to tell me
I am anyone no one wants me to be
wole says ink is a
confectionery expression of my feelings to no one
gwen brought to my attention
simple truths are the demise of anyone
dorothy pointed out
while a perfect rose is paltry to her,
it's good enough for anyone,
good enough for me

Making Room For Love

Reconstruct
Can't self-destruct
Some assembly required
Disbelieve
You feel for me
Selfishness retired
Accepting this
Un emptiness
More difficult than shown
Throw away
My fears and say
These bounds are all but known
Overcome
This endless numb
My hatred does consume
But through love and trust
We can thrust
Out hate to make more room

How You're Loving Me

Empty liquid sugar
Filling me up
Hating how you're
Loving me
Falling into the
Rising hopes, emotions
Burning to say how you're
Cooling me down
Breaking into a
Healing habit
Happy to say that the
Sadness has lessened
Sharing myself and my
Selfish being
Feeling things I was too
Numb to feel
Laughter has dissipated my
Crying spells
Waking to your
Sleeping eyes
Loving how you're
Loving me

Confetti Party

Confetti party
Bright colors in my hair
You make life better

Perfection

I love you;
You are perfect.
Every mistake you've ever made,
Every wrong turn you've ever taken-
I love it all
Because you made them,
Because you took them.
Perfection does not exist,
But my definition does.
We are all human,
We all mess up.
But to me, your "flaws" are infallible.
But to me, your sins are sinless.
But to me, everything you are is
Simply
Defining
Perfection.
No one else can be you;
So, you are
Perfect
For
Me.

5 Senses

I want to gouge out my eyeballs
Put them in a jar with a pretty little bow on top
And set it on your front porch
        -So you can see just how beautiful you are from my
point of view
I want to lose my sense of smell after being
Wrapped in your arms and inhaling your fabric softener
        -So the last scent I ever smelled was yours
I want to pluck the taste buds off my tongue
Right after kissing you
        -So the bitter taste of you is all I remember
I want to burn my skin so badly
That I can't feel a thing
        -So I never have to feel how lifeless everyone else's
touch is
But I don't want to lose my hearing
Because I never want to forget your voice

Two Paths, One Choice

01
imagine if

all the fields in the world were lined up right next to
each other
and we had our pick of which we wanted to lay in
which we wanted to sleep in
and which we wanted to count the stars in
you know none of them would match your beauty

02
what if

you took my hand and led me somewhere
like the beach and we were tucked away
in a secluded place where no one would find us
and we could just smile at each other and be happy
we were alive

03
why can't

things be simpler with our fingertips touching
and your frame against mine
with me brushing the hair out of your eyes

04
because

I'm simply a mess that just doesn't know what to do
anymore
Because where does one go when both roads
Are where she wants to be

Late

I apologize for running late
It seems I've lost my mind
That's not the only thing I've lost
I'm losing grasp of time
Something deep inside of me
Cannot figure out
How to deal with moving life
So I'm left in swirling doubt
After I get buried slowly
Under pounds and pounds of pain
I'll be sure to try so very hard
To tackle tasks and keep myself sane
In response to these words
Like a large black hole
The avarice contained in me
Will start to eat me whole

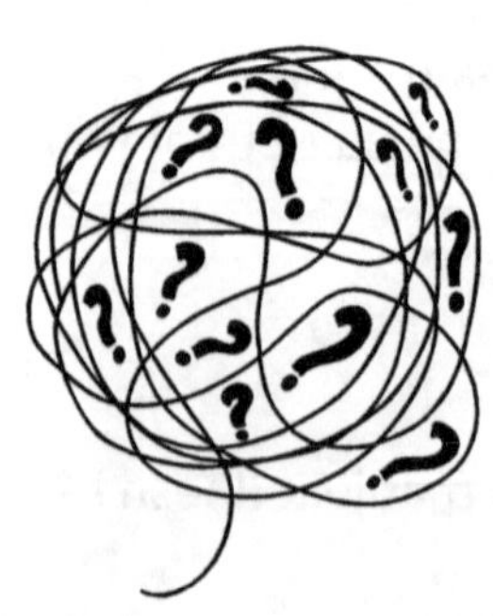

Mood Swings

I don't even know who I am anymore-

Her voice is smooth and repetitive
Humming her own tune
I miss her like I miss the gaping
Wounds deep within my skin

I like saying her and she, it makes me feel
So happy inside as if she were all mine.
[But I know that's a lie]

So where have I been?
That's a good question because I can't even tell you
I can't even tell myself
My thoughts won't let me go
And this may just be a side effect
But my moods are swinging tonight

And for the past couple of days
I also haven't taken my medicine
Until now.
And I'm shakyshaky wishing you were here
By my side
Breathing rapidly to lull me to sleep
With your arm around my chest
As I breathe in and out
You can feel my life expand

And sometimes I get out of character, slip up
And say you instead of she
By then it's impossible to tell who I really mean.

I Am Purposeless

Dear god,
Why do you put me through so much pain
when you know I'm not strong enough for it?

How can you stand to let me scrape metal parts
across my skin until thick watery substance
pours from the opened vein?

What makes you think that I can handle
being in love with two people at the same time?

Who told you it was okay
to let me stay up at night and scream into the empty
dark open sky with no stars to lighten the way?

Where do you think I'll turn to when I realize
she's gone forever
and I'm too late for him to forgive me?

When will it become clear
that I wasn't made for this pain
and I wasn't fit for whatever purpose you may have
forgotten to give me?

Things Are Different

Hello there,
Things are different now
How have you been doing?
Are you happy? Show me how!
And you're invited to my life,
But I urge you not to come
Or I might be reminded
Of things I've left undone;
Of emotions that I've locked
So very far away,
I'd be torn between two loves
And my heartbeat would delay.
It's like I have two rhythms
Flowing through my veins;
Two separate entities
Which occupy my brain

Rainbow Scarf

I've been knitting you a rainbow scarf for quite a while now
A couple years if I remember correctly
Ironic, huh? Because when I started I didn't fully know
I was in love with you yet.

It lays unfinished in my self-soothing room
The only thing that's out of place there
Because it brings me painful memories

If I ever get around to finishing it
Ever feel up to thinking about you
And crying while I'm sitting, knitting
I'll only have to burn it

Because I could never give it away
Like I gave away my heart
And I only gave that away because
I didn't know I was worth your time

I'll hook little flame-retardant hearts
To the edges of the scarf
So when I light it up and the flames consume it
The hearts will remain

Because I will always love you

And that will never change

Do You

I resist the urge to question your motives.
If I give in, it means that I'll show this,
This, unwanted massive wretch of need;
The clingy hungry growing seed
You planted deep inside of me
When you tried to set me free.
Unbeknownst to your mind,
I think about you all the time.
I switch from greed and constant doubt,
And strong emotions I can't let out;
Tumbling turmoil in my head,
Constant playback of what you said-
Both good and bad, running through.
Pathetic? Yes. I need you-
Something I detest to feel,
Yet helps me be somewhat real.
Because I am constant, drifting-
A cloudy weight that's never lifting,
A deep dark black blue clot,
Wishing my mind would finally rot,
So I could make my escape
From the thoughts that have their way,
And pester, control, and hate my brain,
Forcing me to see my veins
From another point of view,
And makes my inner contents spew,
And tells me that you lied to me
When you said that you loved me.
It spurs this rapid, obsessive hate,
Taunting me at an alarming rate.
Swirling thoughts of instant dread,
I lay awake and think in bed
My limbs, so heavy, like iron lead
Pleading for the pain to end.

How Can You Love Me?

How can you love me
When I feel so worthless?
How can you love me
When I love you, love you not?
I pick you like a flower's petals
Pluck, pluck, pluck, pluck
What's best for me?
Suffocation via pillow
Pills, they can't make it down
Not when I wrap this thought around my mouth
So nothing can make its way through
Sadly enough it also covers my ears
So your words do not even come close
Stubborn, obstinate, all of those words
I am, I am, I am
Objectified and helpless
You hold me at such high stakes
I'll let you down
And you will never
Love me the same

Almost

I never get too attached to people
Only objects, like razor blades,
And feelings, like this empty,
Blank, dark abyss that's eating
Through my insides
And lays thick around my heart
I never get too attached to people
Only actions, like vomiting,
And emotions, like this deep,
Dank depression I've let
Suck me dry for the longest time
But I got too attached to you
And it almost made me stop
My empty hopeless feelings,
The deep broken emotions,
The sharp items and regurgitation
Almost.

How This Could End

My lips split right when I started thinking about you
Oh, who am I kidding, I never stopped thinking about you
But I can taste the blood now
And its rusty iron scent reminds me of a worse time
When we both shared scars and arm warmers
It's almost been two months
Since I last sliced open my skin to reveal my inner workings
My hands are cold and my eyes are drooping
As I think of how this could end

Something That I've Missed

Tempting
Twisted metal between my fingertips
I try to hide these secrets
Behind my closed lips
Shut and lock the door
To indulge in my wish
Oh this twisted metal
Is something that I've missed

I Dare You

I dare you to reject me
To detect the truth
And let your cerebral cortex vomit
Hoarse words
That have significant meaning
All over my wretched twitching body

"Your love is like acid
And it's sinking into my veins
Makes me want to slice them open
And bleed away the pain"

I dare you to look me in the eye
To lie and tell me you don't feel that way
And to let your parietal lobe sense
The way that I touch your face
Gentle but not gentle enough
Because it breaks through your paper-thin skin

"I'm saying this to you because
Someone has to say it some time
If you don't get your act together
Someone will do it for you
And you'll just bleed the pain away"

I dare you to say these words to me
To stare and scream and shout
Just don't hurt me
Like I break your heart

I Am Anathema

Shouting until the echoes
Become hoarse and coarse
In my acid filled throat.
The heaviness is unbearable
And tearing me down.
I breathe, think, feel
Heavy.
Pounding head, nausea:
All feelings I'd sooner like to forget–
Love to forget.

And to think,
When I was gone inside myself
So many times ago,
How I felt never faltered
And it still hasn't.
I just have another feeling
Now.
One that is a little stronger.
But, after all, I am impulsive
And I retch, love, buy, feel impulsively

Obsessively, unwanted
like a passionflower
Bloom, one day, die at the end
Although, it restarts
And, re-tortures me each and
Every day.
I can't turn this off,
No matter how I etch the
Regrets of my love
From heart to body

Never, NEVER have I doubted
What I felt.
I put myself on automaton
Just so I could numb the malaise.
In a trance, my life became
So wrapped around one simple
Substance. You.
I morphed the emotions,
made them more acceptable.
Must everything I feel be two?

unmitigated self-
loathing, to the point of
Nearly self-phobic.
Yes, it's self-afflicted, although
beliefs are built around
The words we're immersed in.
My facts aren't always straight
And neither is my repugnant mind
I loved, love, and will continue
to plague myself with this guilt, doubt, and love

Let Myself

Let myself
Feel
Let myself
Be
Content with this nonsense
Let myself
Think
Let myself
Breathe
You in completely
Let myself
Love
Let myself
Show you how vulnerable I am

I will not

Let myself
Do all these things
Because as soon as I do
You will leave

Guilty

Guilty, guilty, GUILTY
The word scrawls itself
Upon my skin, eyes, and brain
I know no other word
Just guilty all the same
No matter how I scream
Or throw myself around
The word will not leave
Its permanent shroud
Buried too deep inside
My distraught mind
To escape
Its claw-like grip scrapes
My heart
Making it hard to breathe
Falling into the trap
You made so easily

Buds

Little nervous petals start
To bloom deep inside of me
Twisting their stems to cause
Uproar in my body
The once-in-a-while thorn pops
At my nerves resulting in
Twitching hand movements,
Jittery legs, and racing thoughts
The leaves reach out
Dragging their edges on blue veins
I'm short of breath here
With only flowers to blame

Anoxia

I am a swamp
Where ideas sink and thoughts overstay,
Bogged down by the muck of my mind
I try to speak, try to release
Some of the stagnant, muddy feelings
But only emptiness seeps out,
So no one knows
I'm really not a crystal spring
Flowing with fresh water on a sunny day
I am a swamp
And my lungs are
Filled with sludge

Pointless

Blink blink blink
My eyes are dry
And sunken in
Every time I look at you
I think think think
My heart is empty
And broken in
I used it once
And let it go
And someone brought it back
So I used it twice
And tore it up
And now I have a shard
Too sharp to not hurt
But too small to make a difference
Restricted welts
Closing in
Burning, itching cut
Nothingness
Emptiness
Void
Null
Moot
Pointless
Hey, hey you, you can't fix me.

Wondering

These feelings are mute,
A dull roar in my chest.
Wondering why I feel this way.

I can almost hear your soft voice
A silhouette against a backdrop
And I wonder why I'm here

Can you tell me how I managed
To stray; running through glass
Wondering why my feet are sore, bleeding

Cutting into my being, the
Guilt is sinking its claws into this touchy flesh
I wonder why it doesn't hurt

I'll let you know when
You fly away
Wondering why you ever stayed.

Bleed

The mosquito bites on my leg
Itch so bad that I might need to
Scratch them so hard that they
Bleed
The look in your eyes
Cuts to bad that I might need to
Hurt myself so much that I
Bleed
But she's got wide-open arms
Waiting for me so long that I
Won't touch the blade or
Bleed

Grateful

I'm grateful for razor blades and the relief
Their sweet kisses bring me
I'm thankful for toothbrushes and gag reflexes
To keep me somewhat skinny
I'm happy that alcohol
Numbs the tears streaming down my face
I'm glad the drugs can
Take your place

I'm upset the knives don't
Embrace me enough
I'm sorry throwing up
Is getting too tough
The alcohol stings
As it goes down
But I'm happy through
All this you've stuck around

Infallibly Flawed

The music flows in my ears
And doesn't exactly do its job
Of running her out of my mind
She is grey-blue pieces of glass
That I cut myself on when I step too hard,
Too far in the sandy depths of the ocean.
Because she is the feeling I have when I am weightless
Floating on the salty current
And she reminds me of every slow piano song I hear
And the sweet voice of the boy
Who sings to me about his first love
I could listen to that song for hours
Each time it gets more powerful
And I get more pathetic.
Where do I go tonight
She is reasons not to hurt
And also reasons why
She is the stinging feeling
On my wrist right now
And the heaviness in my heart when I look in the mirror
And picture her face right next to mine
She is rustling of papers and plastic bags
That keeps me awake at night
When I am sleepy-eyed
And in another world
Simply so, she is just
Infallibly flawed.

Just Keep Walking

I can hear the pit-pat
Of your jean legs swiping
Each other as you walk on by

You just keep walking

I can taste the sweat
Drop on your lip slipping
Down, salty on your tongue

You just keep walking

I can feel the magnetic
Pull from your heart, the
One that wants to yell
"Don't walk away" but

You just keep walking

And now I see what
It really means to be

Alone.

Grey Lined Walls

My face tightens and gets soggy wet
as I wonder if this is the way life will always be
so-called-empty threats
followed by so-called-friends emptying
and strolling hand in hand
to the sunset and away from the
desperate bleeding corpse of nothing-girl

and I somehow doubt their thoughts will linger
on this pile of pathetic absence
every-so-often I imagine they will look back
and remember lousy-excuse-for-a-being
and sweep her way out of sight out of mind out of thoughts
because what is this fragmented child to them?

Yet I know that if any were in this situation
I'd be strong there for them
never once get vexed and sure I'd be frustrated
why can't you see that we care?
But I would always be so standing stable waiting
for the day that they got better
and we could wander off and celebrate
in pajamas with our favorite form of almost-high

but I'm not them and I know that I've hurt them
one too many times
for me to take any of it back
and I'm so sick of saying sorry
that I can only say it to myself anymore
can only say it to the one that I hate the most

so I'm forced to sit here
soaking from the tear ducts down
waiting for some sweet relief to take me upupup and away
from here
'cause life's looking dull and grey
with shades of rainbow in-between
like the way my fingers were supposed to be wrapped in-
between the spaces of yours

sometimes the solitude is much too silent.

Her and Him

I want to tuck you away
Close to my heart
And carry you around like I carry my book of poems
I've got so many words swirling around all thoughts
of you
And they intertwine and whisper to me
They let me know long ago that I was in love with
you the first year I ever met you
There was something special about you that I just
couldn't let go
And I'm glad I didn't because you were my first love

I want to show you off
To the whole world
And keep you next to me forevermore
I've got so many thoughts of you, dreams of you,
and love for you
That they just overflow and mix and mold
It took a while for these feelings to develop
But I'm so glad that they did
I'm so glad you were persistent
Because without that perseverance on your behalf
I'd be cold and alone without my last love

Second Chance

I hate you
Because I'm hurt
I hate myself
Because I always have
I'm mad at you
Because I'm hurt
I'm mad at myself
Because I let you go

I wish you would understand enough
To give me another chance

Missing You

Sometimes I wake up in the morning
And it just hurts so much
That I am immobilized for a few
Moments in time

Sometimes I stay awake at night
Because it hurts so much
As the tears fall down my face
And I scream empty silence into pitch-black room

I miss you
And that's all there is.

3 poems in one

Bathe in	The beauty
Creativity	And love
That makes	You hold
Things dear	Is what life means
To you	A blessing
And	A curse?
Take and	Or
Keep life as	Both.
If you were	Anything like
Delicate, fragile,	You would be
Easy to break.	Unheard of
Like your heart	Your feelings
Are too	Much like
Many twisters.	Natural disasters
That	Destroy any-
One or	Thing.
More people	Live and
Die from	The pain
Consuming the heart.	Will
You	Be
A girl who is getting	Over
The message that	Eventually
Breaks your heart?	Die
Another day	And it
Will not stop it	Will not end

This is my life
Bipolar.

What I Once Believed

I Don't Treat You Right

I don't treat you right
I've got sugarcoated lies
And I'm never satisfied
With where I am or what I'm doing, no
My sweater smells exactly
The way she tastes
And I just push you away
Like I watched her fall away from me
And into the arms of someone else.

I don't treat you right
I've got you hypnotized
But you've got to realize
I'm not who you think I am, no
My tears taste exactly
The way her touch felt
And I just tuck my feelings under my belt
Like the way you tuck me in at night
And fold me up in your arms.

I don't treat you right
A little piece of me dies
As the guilt inside me tries
To make me say no
My music sounds exactly
The way she laughed
And I just let it pass
Like I let her go
Like I let you go

You're gone.

Everyone's Leaving

Somehow I wish I could have been there
Like you are for her
But those shooting stars are all empty now
Because I never said
'Anything'
And I'm stuck in over and over land
Where I just repeat the same scene
Over and over
Until my mascara runs down my cheeks
And stains them a licorice-black
Not the toughest eye-makeup remover
Could get rid of
So my sadness will turn me cold
And my chills will shift my scars from puce to purple
And that will be more of a reminder
Why you left me

Truly Happy

i.
This is the third night in a row
That I've dreamt about you
I woke up crying the first night because
You told me you still loved me
How I wish that were true

ii.
I'm keeping myself awake with energy shots
And bad television just to keep you
Out of my sleep [that's where I'm supposed to be content]
The second night all I remember was taking in your
Sweet embrace

iii.
But I don't think I can hold off on rest any longer
I've got a big trip ahead of me
And I've got to keep my head held high
The third night we sang and laughed and danced
And I was truly happy

Not Right

My choice was for the better [worst]
My decision made me better [worse]
I am [un]happy with what I've done
I'm simply in heaven [hell]
How can I feel so good [bad]
How can I [not] be able to breathe?
Knowing everything I did to you
Was so unacceptable
There is no other option
It's just wrong
And it's never going to be right

Dusky Tears

She's so beautiful
 But she's gone now

I thought things would be okay
But then I saw photos of her

And it's nighttime now
And all my daytime anger has dissipated
Into dark dusky tears

Swept at
Your feet

Before

I immersed myself into the sun
And burned all my friends along the way
Such a silly thought, to be the one
Stuck forever night while he is forever day
I ignited the lantern with so much care
And so much time it took me still
All my friends vanished in thin air
To leave me forever at darkness' will
The flames consumed my very heart
And turned me away from the others
We act as if we're miles apart
All because I chose my lover

Just Wishes

I get my expectations up
That for just a moment there'd be a time
When you'd remember you are mine
And I am yours
But I guess that I was wrong
And I'm singing the same song
Wishing you could somehow miss me
But I never understood
Why I spend so much time alone
And you are always home
With someone else
Disappointment's coursing through
And my final speech is due
I'm giving it to you
And there's nothing left to do
You don't miss me
But you wish you did
And I wish you could
But that's all they are
Just wishes.

Dear Anyone

Dear girl,
Sometimes it gets so lonely at 4:00 in
The morning
When there's not one person around
That I can talk to about
How much I miss her

Dear boy,
I wish you were awake right
Now
So I could whisper to you
That I love you and I can dab at my tears
And say
I don't miss her, I don't miss her

Dear anyone,
If you're even listening
I'm just going to tell you ahead of time
You're going to hurt in this life
You're going to miss someone

Far Away

Staring out the window
While the tip tap of the rain
Keeps me company
I'm wracking my brain trying to find answers
For the reasons I left you for someone else
I know the rationale behind it
And yet I can't help but blame myself
I love you and I'm still hurting
But I bet I'm all erased from your heart now
So I'll be on my way
Far, far away

Looking Back

I look back on all your old poems
And it somehow makes more sense now
And even though this was months ago
Tears still come tumbling down
And I want to count to a number that will make your
Pain go away and never relocate to a place you can see
Because if you can see it,
I can feel it and it just digs into me and kills me inside
I don't want your twenty-seven stitches
And your stupid three-inch scars
I measure them myself with a pocket ruler
Oh and oh, my head just aches right now
Because my mother is in the other room
And I can't cry in front of her
Especially not over you
No one truly gets this
And not even you understand how much I love[d] you
I wish I could infuse the feelings into your mind
So you realize that you were worth all the pain
I suffered through when I tried to get close to you
And you just pushed and pushed me away
But now I want to say that you're not and weren't anything
But that would be a lie
Because I love you more than you will ever know
And I will continue to bleed your name out of my system
Until the pain doesn't come anymore

I Never Lied

So I let go of you
And all the memories your
Barbed little Polaroid camera spit out
And into your bony hand
So I've forgotten what color your eyes are
And everything you've wanted to become
But I won't forget the pain
And I can't forget the love
So I've started to erase your
Presence from my mind
And I'm trying to purge you from my system
So I don't remember what it feels like
To be next to you on grassy plains
And hovering above you
In fields in mid-afternoon
I've got nothing to save

Isolation and Drugs

These demons have got control
They take you under and pull you away
From everything you've ever known to be safe in this world
And you let them.
They coax you forth with their delusive words
About how much better you'll feel with them
And how much you'll spiral down without them
But the truth is, you'll be spiraling either way
And all they really do is isolate you from the world
Don't count on me to pick you back up
When your shaky limbs, nosebleeds, and poisoned scars
Knock you to the ground

Trying to Sleep

I'm high because of
Seroquel and Abilify
All mixed up with Ambien
Trying to get myself to sleep
Slipped me up into perpetual
Hallucinations and tripping over
My own two feet
Let me know when you get there too
Because I'll meet you in the middle
Although you're high because
You want to be
I guess this relationship in question
Is really nothing more than
My own thoughts bantering back and forth
Inside my head
Because in reality
I guess there was never anything in the first place.

Looking for Words

I didn't try to take back the warmth
That I left at your side
And I swear I swear I'm trying
But I know this will get me nowhere
Because I'm nothing but empty excuses
And attempts at making myself feel all right
When I know all I really want is for you to feel
More than all right
More than just fine
I want to take back those twenty seven pretty
Stitch marks, your handy work
I want to make you return them to the devil
Who whispered those thoughts into your head
In the first place
And you're right; my hand isn't reaching down to pull you up
Because I'm already at the bottom
Waiting to catch you

Breaking Your Own Bones

It was never about the
Fields or the kissing for hours
It was never about the words
Or the way they hurt and healed
It was about the way you made me feel
And now it's about the way you don't make me feel
It's about all the ways you're hurting yourself
And how much I don't want to endure that
And how much I'd love for you to be cured
Fixed, completely whole again
It's about your life and how you live it
It's not about me ever, please
And I hope to god you hear my words
Hear my pleas and take them to heart
Because how can you be unbroken
If you're constantly breaking your own bones?
You're not going to be happy
If you won't let anyone contribute to it.

P
u
r
e

L
u
c
k

I'm curled up on my side
In the back of your shiny
Silver ride hoping you won't notice
How I'm whimpering from time
To time; hoping you won't notice
Me at all
Because I'm not supposed to be here
And I think I let the glass slip
Through my bony fingers, sliding bloodied
Down to the ground for my feet
To step on
Crunch
And now I'm picking up the shattered pieces
Trying hopelessly to put them together
When all I needed was to need you
And never forget that
But I somehow forgot the meaning
Like an infant just learning words.

I put the memories in a heart shaped box
With blue fur on the top
Even the things I stole from you
That you don't know about
And I put it away and if fur could collect dust well
It would be dustier than an antique shop
That closed last February

And I lost the back of my phone
And the only thing keeping it from falling apart
Is pure luck
Because the battery is open and waiting to
Crash to the ground
I take this as a sign
Because I lost it somewhere between
Losing you and entering a new life
And the only thing that's
Holding me together
Is pure luck

Sit Hope Crush Cold: Winter's Raging On

Time ticks slowly by
I put my earbuds in one by one
Look outside at the white-out sky
And smile; yet still I'm unsatisfied
A shadow rolls across my page
My heart skips a beat, hoping
It's you
Should've stopped, not skipped
Because you weren't there
Turn my music up, drowning out hope
Wiping the smile off my face as
New buds spring from the earth
Through clumpy crystal snow
Like the wisp of movement
I feel in the air, emerging with
Another beat-skipper
Should've realized
Winter's not over yet

You Were Here and Now You're Gone

I saw you in the night
And tried to hold you in my arms
But you slipped straight through
And only left me scars
I haven't heard of you since then
Now I only feel pain
You were once my friend
But things are not the same

Pencil to Pen

I'm writing in pen now,
A more permanent resolution
To my once temperamental state
I know what I want now
And it's no longer selfish
I can no longer hurt you
And I no longer plan to
I intend to let you decide
What's best for both your lives
And oh, to God I pray
You choose to live your way
If that means separating from
All I've ever known
I'm ready to let you fly
And stay far from home
Darling dear I love you
I always, always will
And now I'm letting go for you
Yet I'm holding on a little still

Pushed You Away

Day01
You're smiling more
You grab my hand and I just don't want to let go

Day02
I can hear the whistling of the blue jay
And the rushing of the waves on the ocean
And I remember what it's like to hold you

Day03
Sadness overwhelms me as I think about
The boy I left behind for the life
That I wanted to build, even if it was for a moment.
With you

Week02
We're talking less
I grab my phone and I just want you to answer me

Week03
I can hear the screeching of nails on chalkboard
And the crashing sound of glass all around
And I remember what it's like to miss you

Week04
It's been a month now
And things were wonderful
I let you have my heart
And I told you to give yours away
So you did.

Day35
It's over now and I'm br-bro-broken
But it doesn't matter because I'm the one
Who pushed you away
In the first place.

Increments of Three

It's two in the morning
And we're talking about cereal
And I'm thinking just how much I love you

It's two oh one in the morning
And I'm writing my tenth poem for the day
And I'm thinking how much pain I must be in

It's two oh two in the morning
And I'm typing faster than the minutes can go by
Because increments of three just plain suck

It's two oh three in the morning
And I wish they didn't come threes
And I wish they didn't come at all

You, Me, and Pain

Oh how you can take something so sweet
So innocent
And twist turn it into something vile
That I never want to touch again

Did I tell you this, yet?
I'm moving somewhere far away from here
Where I can sit under willow trees
And write for hours at a time.

And did I fail to mention that
No matter what, you won't be able to reach the trunk
Of my willow, because if you could
You would surely turn it black.

My hair will grow long like it once was
And when it turns 5:08
I'll remember I wrote this poem and think about how
I really do miss the way you break hearts
And everything in between.

There will be a garden of nothing but
Forget-me-nots
Because please, don't forget me
I want you to remember my tear-stained face
And all those ugly lies you told me
When you thought it would be cool to play
With my fragile aluminum heart.

The heart that you tore a piece out of
Just in time for me to get a check up
To make sure I'm running all right
And just my luck
They notice how it's not quite right
Because in actuality, it looks as if there is a hole
The size of a pencil straight through the middle-
The vital part.

Oh how you take something so sweet
So innocent
And make it so I can't think about it
Without thinking of you, me, and pain.

I Am Broken

I Am
>Thinking of you in the morning and wish my alarm clock wasn't

Broken
>So I could wake up in time to see the smile on your face as you
>make your way

Alone
>To your workplace. I love it when you come home after I've
>been waiting

And waiting
>To fold you up in my arms. You bring me flowers, but they're
>wilting and about

To die
>Maybe the sunlight will show that they're really alive and
>things aren't how they seem to be.

First Love

Through my ups and downs
You were there
You mattered more than my own life
You were my life
But now you are drifting
Away, too far away
And I shed tears of discomfort
When I think of the pain
And how much it hurts when you're gone

Through my love and my [self] hate
You were there
You helped me live when I no longer wanted to
You were my life
But now you are detaching
From me, too far away
And I weep, paralyzed for hours
When I think of the love
And how great it felt when you were here

Through my sanity and insanity
You were there
You brought my life back to reality
You were my life
But now you are distant
So far away, too far away
And misery consumes me
When I think of the haze
And how much I loved you, but you've gone away

But you've gone away.
And that's how we'll stay.
First love
Still love
Pain, hurt, love
Love

Without You

Can I really be nothing but
Wispy movements in the air?
Can I really fade along the lines of the horizon
And change colors to match the pink orange sky
When I really need to fly away from it all?

I imagine that I try so hard to accomplish
This idea
I twirl and swirl it in my head
Like glitter in a pool of water
Never forming perfect circles
But still creating beauty all the same

So I'll write and write and write again
Until I get these thoughts clear out
Of my head and onto paper
So I can coherently feel and think
Without you.

Leave it at That

I can taste the salty mess of water in my mouth
Because it slips through the cracks in my chapped lips
Without those several flavors of ChapStick, you know,
the ones I gave you for Christmas last year, I'm just
bite, pick, bleeding
And thinking about you
We're all different now
And I don't believe I'll ever get over your
Wavy hair, lengthy and strong
Or your sweet eyes hidden behind glasses and layers
of tresses
I'll always remember the way you drew
And how you paint
And I love the way you attempt to sing
But I'm here now
And you're there
So I'll just remember, cry, and leave it at that

Unwoven.

One day we'll look back on this and
Realize we are no longer a "we"
We are two separate entities
No longer woven together like we wanted to be

One day I'll look back on this and
Be able to not cry, weep, sob out my feelings
Onto the shoulder of a broken boy who
Breaks a little more each time I shed a tear over you

One day you'll look back on this and
Know how right you were to end all the
Bullshit right where you did because
I'm not the right girl for you

But for right now, I will always
Think and breathe things involving you
And stab myself with your simple three-letter name
The curves of the letters
Are so smooth against the paper
But the meaning of the word
And the pain behind it
Lends it all the sharpness it needs
But I'll be just fine when you're gone
It'll just take some years and tears
Before that happens.

For A Reason

It's chilly outside
And I think of your
Thrift-store drug-rug
That keeps you warm
In the wind

This room is rather cold
And my math teacher
Explains simple algebra
But I can only think of
How smart you are

I'll be walking from this class
And out into the brisk air
Wrapping my very own drug-rug
Tight around my body
Exactly where your arms should be

Then I'll get home
And feel warm, smiling
Knowing that I can be happy
Just as long as you are
You found each other for a reason

A Load of Laundry

I'm sitting on the dryer
Waiting for the washing machine to
Stop churning, twisting, tugging
On my soaking wet clothing
I'm in my pajamas with damp hair
And a note in my pocket
It says 'I love you so much'
With a little heart scribbled in the bottom left corner
I hear the clunk thud signifying the end of the cycle
And I quickly move all my shirts, pants, and underwear
To the cool metal frame of the dryer
I know you're not supposed to wash them together
But I'm the kind of person who wants it done now
And when I get something in my head,
It takes more than anyone's might to get it out
Like when I wanted to die
Nothing but the attempt could snap me out of it
Like when I wanted you
Nothing but being with you could get you out of my mind
But now I'm not wishing waiting anymore for you
Because I feel so content that you've moved on
I couldn't get over the pain
If you hadn't first

The Seasons

The humidity is rising, dear
And it reminds me of the way
You made my palms sweaty
As the sunlight cascaded down
From the sky and all around
Your magnificent smile.

But my hands are ice cold now
Like the way you stare
Right at me,
Right through me.
And it seems that
No matter which way I turn,
The bitter taste of you
Is always at the
Back of my throat
And the tip of my tongue.

The seasons are starting to change
Though and I'll be trading in my
Thoughts of you for a warm
Sweater to shield me from
The chill of autumn's hand
Which is big enough to wrap
Around my shoulders and infest
My very being with rotten colors
And moldy thoughts like
The ones I'm thinking right now,
"I miss you"
So I'll close my window and turn
On my fan to drown out the heat
And muffle my thoughts, even
If it's only for a little while

When winter rolls around I'll be
Shivering because there aren't enough
Blankets in the world to keep your cold
Lips from whispering in my head
And not even melted snow can
Wash away the putrid colored stains
On my lungs from when I ate, slept,
And breathed you.

Spring will sneak in and I'll find myself
Picking petals: loves me, loves me not
But will always end on half a petal
Broken like the time you shattered glass
For the heck of it. Landing somewhere
In between loves me and not.

And before I know it, a whole year
Of seasons will go by that will have been
Sans you.

This can only get easier in the end.

Midday Interruption

I've got a mind worth losing, so tell me why I can't
Shake the feeling that you've already heard this rant
And don't forget the fact that I've got to take these pills
To get my fill of neurological vitamins
But I can't stand the sight of them
But I'm not right without them
They can't cure my sins, what I've said or where I've been
But the lies are wearing thin
-yes I swear I took them!
A midday interruption, which is slightly counterproductive
An alarm to remind me to be calm
Three little pills fit perfectly on my palm
Tick Tock watch the clock, can't remember what I forgot
Getting better was worth a shot
But maybe I just thought I ought to get well faster
Recovery's a disaster. I've learned how to master
Tellin' people I'm fine and they believe I'm not lyin'
But I'm still wondering why I'm
Spending so much time using my efforts hiding instead of
trying
Big sigh back track to the everyday medication,
An unofficial invitation to a psychological conversation
I'm still waiting, losing patience for this stigma loving nation
Your illness is not the focus, the joke is, everybody knows this
Is make believe, a made-up disease used for sympathy
Excuse me?
This is sick; how so many believe the lies, ignore the cries, but
these are the times
Where we need to scream, show them what it means
To never have dreams. To only be filled with nightmares
Living in a world that's not fair
Who cares? You there!
Oh dear, sorry that I'm shouting again
I forgot to take my medicine
Eight o clock on the dot
There's no harm in the alarm but I forgot-got-got.

Stress

I am climbing a mountain
But an avalanche stops me halfway
And wipes away all progress

I am swimming the ocean
But a tsunami stops me halfway
and sweeps me back to shore

I am scaling a skyscraper
But an earthquake stops me halfway
And shakes me to the ground

I am biking cross country
But a tornado stops me halfway
And twist-turns me around to the start

I am doing, seeing, experiencing, living
And when I get stopped halfway
I must remember, stress may be natural but it
doesn't have to be a disaster

Eyelashes

The smoke swirls in my eyelashes
And twisty-turns upward to dance around in
my side-swept bangs
And my short-short hair is bouncing as I run
Away from you because you swore you'd
Go crazy if I made this more than just a habit

The salty water specks escape through my lashes
And slide slowly down my cheek red and raw
Down down down it goes until it drip drops
Onto my carnelian arm
You swore you'd always be there for me
Until the end of fucking time

And these eyelashes are getting worn out
As the many shed and are laying someplace
Upon your fingertips from you brushing the tears away
Oh, I knew you would go crazy, I just didn't know you'd stay

Away From the Edge

I have been at the edge
Not once, not twice, but four times
I failed, I failed, I failed, failed
The first time my stomach got me
The second was guilt
The third was burning pain
And the fourth, love
Which I would have never experienced
If I weren't such a failure
If I didn't get so queasy
If I hadn't felt so guilty
If I never stood up to the bad taste, burning liquid death,
fiery poison, and seething welts.
But I was, I did, I had, and I fought the urge to
Keep the flow of bottled hurt
Down down down my throat
Fighting between such and the
Horrid stinging on my tongue
So I let you in and when
It came to my leap off the
Edge, you grabbed my shaky
Hand and never let go.
I pushed and pushed away
I said things I shouldn't say
I wept and shook and you,
You stayed.
Now, I'm a little
           Further from
                The edge

Sweat and Tears

I
Somewhere along the way
'I love you too' lost its meaning
And became just another phrase to say
Like 'pass the milk' or 'how are you today?'
And my smiling face became just another façade
For you to get lost behind
Another maze for you to unlock and a puzzle for you
To put together
But I stole a piece from the box
And you can never completely make it whole

II
Somehow I let the words 'love you'
Become empty and powerless
When they evoke such powerful emotion
Almost all of the time
How did I get so lost in this world?

III
No I won't let this happen any longer,
I'm going to put the meaning back into those simple words
Even if it means I have to crawl
Through dirt and blood
And sweat and tears

50 Miles Between Us

I like the way red flannel looks against your skin,
The way your smile brings out mine
And the way you accept me with my sin.
In my self-destructive battle, you've been there
standing strong
You know, I can really count on you
And I've done it all along.
It may not have seemed that way at times, but our
friendship is so true
That even with the arguments,
We will always make it through.
My scars depict a battle, and you always show you care
How did I survive before we met?
And before you were always here?

My Someone

These scars on my wrist are a timeline
Of the pain I went through in the past
They're white and almost healed now
To show that my pain will not last
Scars are a thing of beauty,
They show that the suffering's done
When they're healed I'll have a story
A story that might save someone.
I value your life so dearly
I cling to the breaths that you take
I pray you don't leave me alone here
If not for yourself then for my sake.
The unhappiness may consume you
But it doesn't last forever
You'll make it through this I swear
I'll stand by you, we'll do this together
The end may seem near
But your story has only just begun
I promise I will be here,
You are my someone.

Repression

My memory is lacking
And I feel intense opposites
First, I feel the endless need for you
Next, I feel something
From long ago
Something lurking in the realm
Of the unknown
Will I ever remember?
Or will I continue to feel worthless
Pointless, useless
Afterwards?
This is when the hate takes over
And again, I reiterate to you
I cannot love and hate simultaneously
So I love you, then I hate me, then I love you
Then I am unsure
And now here I am
Scared as can be
Has tragedy befallen me
In my lost childhood?
I'm sorry I'm not
What you expected
Please, don't judge me
I never meant it
Never meant to be neutral to you
And bring back the pain
Am I the way I am
Because someone took matters into his or her own hands?
I wish I could become nothing
And crawl under a dark cool rock
So I could slither away
And weep

Sleep

Sleep is like a reset button
For me, anyway
It takes my powerful emotions
And pushes them away
But they always come back, you know
And I'll just go to sleep again
But I don't want to sleep my life away
I'm just looking for a friend
To be with me when I'm not asleep
Because life's not worth an hour awake
And I'm living just for him

So Dependent

I spend my life envying
Other people's lives
I'm nothing but a wallflower
Dependent on people to survive
And when they disappear
Because I pushed them away
For them life goes on
But it ends for me that day.

Markers, Milk, and Me

I am the last bit of marker that is dried out and doesn't work
You left the cap off for a week and when you returned,
You threw me in the trash.
I no longer fulfilled my purpose; I became useless to you,
So, you pushed me aside and moved on to your next project.
Soon you have a miniature landfill of markers- all met with the
same fate.

You blame the markers
You blame the ink
You do not blame yourself

I am the last cup of milk that is stagnant and rotten
You let me go past the expiration and when you finally noticed,
You dumped me down the drain.
I no longer brought you nutritional value, only putrid smells
and nauseous emotions
So, you added more to your list for your next trip to the store.
Soon your sink is filled with other gallons and flavors like me.

You blame the milk
You blame the fridge
You do not blame yourself

You used your words and actions against me,
Pouring ink in my glass and forcing me to drink.

I blame the markers
I blame the milk
I blame myself.

No Vacancy

My mind is like a hotel room,
People come and go.
Some linger and stay a while,
Choosing to check out slow.
Others stay for half a night,
Sometimes a day or two.
And others do unspeakable things,
So I can't rebook the room.

His, Hers, and Mine

How dare you call me weak
When I am anything but.
I have been beaten down by
A man's sense of entitlement,
A woman's cruel sense of love,
And my own learned self-loathing.

I've seen the sunset turn red
And tried to imitate its beauty
With my body as the canvas.
Instead of art I created a monster
That feeds off the man's heightened self-worth,
The woman's barbed words,
And my own self-deprecating thoughts.

I look to the moon for guidance now
Because it's easier to hide in the night.
The scars left behind will never see the light of day
I am now a ghost of who I was,
Left to be the nightmare that
He ignores
She suppresses
and I regret.

No Safe Haven

I think I flew away today
Disappeared, I fear
The hold the past has on me
Is evident and clear
I'm often robbed of present day,
By polluted history
And if there is a day I escape
What will become of "me"?
Because who am I,
If not comprised of a compilation
Of my lived experiences
Of trials and tribulations?
Around each bend,
Where there could have been
A corner of safe haven
Instead I was met
Time and again with
Situations more forsaken

Hope

I've overdosed on hope and now
I'm up in the clouds
they're fluffy, soft and
I'm falling through them
my back is to the ground,
my limbs are in the air
and even if I wanted to scream,
I wouldn't be able to
gravity and time are against me
as I plummet down, down, down
the clouds cover the sun
and loom above
any moment earth and body will meet
and just like the clouds,
hope slips through my hands.

Don't Turn Out The Lights

I'm not even going to pretend
That I dreamt I was a lie anymore
As I lay out on the linoleum floor
And sudden realization comes pouring down on me
I've been a lie my whole life
No one caught it before
No one saw through my translucent body
And cut me down right to the hollowed out bone
My last year has been sloppy and broken
So they all could tell what I was
-Or wasn't
They told me I could cry on their shoulders
But when their fingertips slid right through
My gossamer frame
The illusion of me just fell
And it keeps falling faster each day
As more and more people become aware
Of my transparent soul
I am nothing more
Than tracing paper
Hanging from clothes lines
In the incandescent sunshine
I am airy and you can't see me
Anymore

Not Much Time

I'm trying to hold myself together
But I've only got enough thread
For seven stitches straight across my arm
It might not matter anyway-
It seems I've lost the needle
Much like I've lost my mind
I've been unravelling for a decade
Of decayed emotion,
At the edge of the top floor of the clock tower, counting down
The time I've got left
I was fine until I thought about
What happens when it runs out.
Vertigo hits me hard and heavy
And the minute hand has been replaced
By a millisecond finger.
I twirl, I fall, I break.
Time is up.

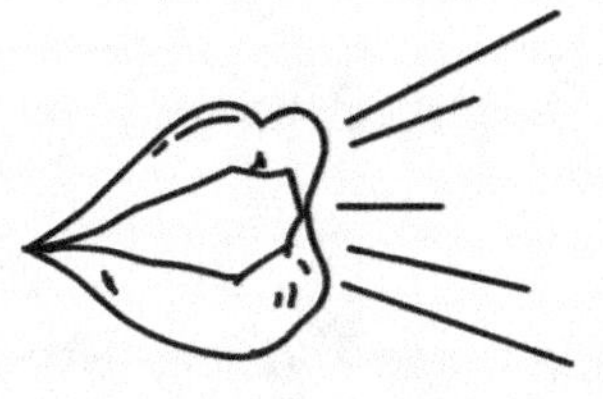

The... End?

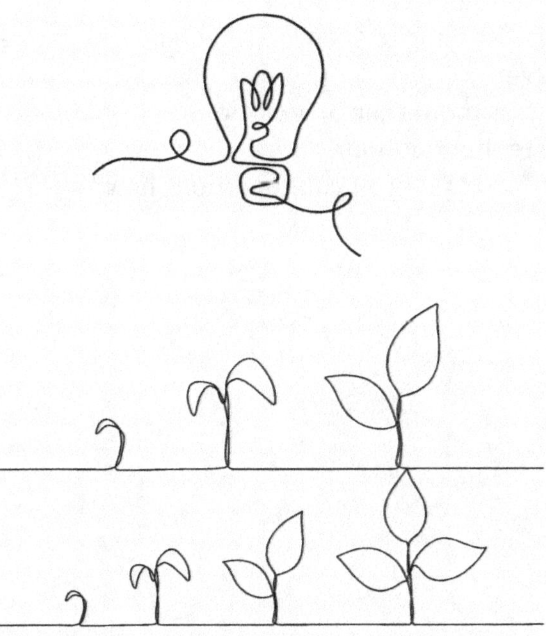

What is Happiness?

Happiness is coming home and seeing the dishes
Piled up that he promised to do.
Happiness is feeling frustrated and upset until
he comes home
Happiness is expressing your feelings on the situation
Happiness is filling the sink with water and soap and
blowing bubbles at each other
Happiness is trying to see who is faster – the washer
or the dryer
Happiness is more than an emotion,
it is a state that fluctuates
-It allows you to feel all your emotions healthily

The Rest of My Life Looks Like Him

People say all kinds of things about love
They say it's floating on air like a happy cloud
They say it is a pleasant dream
That it's a song serenaded in the sunrise
But I think love is not wanting to be sad with anybody else
It's only wanting to be mad at the person wrapping his
hand around your waist as you drift off, lips curling
upward out of sight
It's thinking about love and
being compelled to write this poem
as your screen lights up the blackness and
dilates your eyes
It's smiling in the dark,
knowing that the rest of your life looks like him

Cyclical

I'd like to scoop out the source of this pain
But I'm already hollow enough as it is,
From years of escaping myself...
Until I can't run away anymore
I don't want to face my trauma
Because I can't possibly take any more
But the longer it goes unresolved
The more I will have to face
I'm stuck in this endless cycle
A loop that I can't erase

Too

Have you ever been too?
I too, have been too.
I was born to too,
I grew up as too,
I've been affected by too,
I feel, think, eat, sleep, bleed, too

How Long Has It Been?

A week's gone by
At least, that's what I heard them say
But everything feels the same
Each day still plagued with pain

5 months' gone by
At least, that's what the calendar says
But everything feels the same
Just like the day you came

10 years' gone by
At least, that's what the paperwork says
But everything feels the same
I've got nothing left to gain

3 decades' gone by
At least, that's what the TV says
But everything feels the same
My mind's too hard to train

A whole lifetime's gone by
At least that's what the monitor says
But everything feels the same
I was forged and will die in shame

I thought that things would change
But everything feels the same

The Things That Stayed

I said the things I said
And now they're out there off my chest
And you said that I'd feel better
But I'm emptier instead
If all my words are sacred
And a picture's worth a thousand
But it's painted with my eyes closed
In the closet where you found them
If no one did believe me
And my brain hid it away
Were you all committing blasphemy
While I just played with paint
I guess "your body is a temple"
Is just a sad excuse to prey
And I'm covered in your bruises
But they're hidden tucked away
And all the other children asked
Why don't you come and play
But I've been acting my whole life
Just pretending I'm okay
I've never been myself
And still I'm not today
And if we took away the t
And the paint becomes just pain
And the cross was just a symbol
For grown men to shed their shame
Remorse is for the miserable
It's all just a sick game
Where the players are pathetic
And the victims lose again
And it's rigged from the beginning
And through to the very end
And it just loops forever
A tragic run on sentence
So I said the things I said
And now they're out there off my chest
And you said that I'd feel better
But I'm emptier instead

It Was Only a Dream

I dreamt I was a flower
But when I awoke, I was wilted,
My leaves were dried up,
And my petals were falling to the ground
I dreamt I was a hurricane
But when I awoke, I was only nimbus clouds
With small drops of water
And a gentle breeze
I dreamt I was a bird
But when I awoke, I was surrounded by plucked feathers,
My wings were broken,
And a cage loomed overhead
I dreamt I was beautiful, powerful, and free
But when I awoke, I was still only me.

I Am Just Wishes

I wish I were sunsets on vacation,
Fresh flowers in the garden,
And raindrops on an overly dry day.

I wish I were a gentle breeze in the summer heat,
A refreshing glass of floral tea,
And sunshine on Spring's first day.

I wish I were colorful, crunching leaves on a hike,
A daffodil and daisy crown,
And a rainbow on a stormy day.

But I am blinding rays that sunglasses and
hats can't keep out of your face
I am spreading weeds, crowding out
your beautiful blossoms
I am a flash flood with no time to prepare or escape
I am a tornado crashing through before you can hide away
I am lukewarm disappointment dripping from
the coaster in distaste
I am the chill of winter's touch letting you know
I'm still within reach
I am muddy soil trapping you in place
I am a crown of thorns, broken and bleeding
I am an illusion you don't bother keeping

Forget, Not Forgive

They say to forgive and forget
But I just want to forget
Forget all the pain and what you did to me
Forget all the shame and insecurity

Oil and Water

I'm the kind of tired
That years of sleep do not fix
The kind of tired
How oil and water don't mix

Interstellar

I am far away
And I may have always been
Maybe I was supposed
To be born in another galaxy
Maybe I wasn't supposed
To have been born at all
Either way, my stardust
Isn't enough to keep me here
So I am far away
And I may always be

Layers of Closed Doors

I am sad today
And I've been sad before
But this is some sort of sadness
From layers of closed doors
This is an aching feeling
A familiar and unfamiliar thing
I've felt this in the past-
But when? it echoes when it rings
I just know that last time,
Whenever this occurred,
My actions were to erase myself
And now it has recurred
So now I must stay true to me
Despite the unknown
But it's incredibly difficult to combat
This feeling of being utterly alone

Plausible Deniability

You grind my bones into a paste
You make a salve to save some face
Everyone sees a hero, rescuing the sick
No one peeks behind the curtain, just enamored that
"he's done it!"

A miracle, bridging gaps and caverns
But look at the bodies paving the way,
Revealing a not-so-subtle pattern
You've feigned innocence all because
You "don't do it on purpose"
Assessing all the damage you've caused
Was choosing ignorance worth it?

It Wears My Face

It is within me
It can become me
It puts on my skin,
One bone at a time
Layering my capillaries,
Tendons and muscles-
All falling into place
Gracefully and as if
I was never even there before
It wears my face
It takes my smile
It infuses itself into my marrow,
Slowly replacing me over time
My heart beats as its own
I don't want to be hollow
I don't want to fade
I want to be me
I want to be mine

The Moment

I'm in love with the moment I instantly forgot a thought
As each syllable escaped my brain
Before they could connect to form a full word
They disappeared just the same
Dissipated, never to be thought again

I'm in love with the moment a weight was lifted from my chest
A thought from the past? Anxiety of what's to come?
I will never know, as my brain was temporarily blessed
With the gift to forget the future and what's been done
But it's not that easy to run

I'm afraid of the moment...

And it's not that easy to run

Threadbare

I'm sorry, I am not myself today.
But have I ever been? Who can really say?
I never got the chance to grow and be myself,
I have always lived my life for someone else.
Who am I at all, if I don't live to please?
I've only ever tried to achieve other people's dreams.
The ebb and flow of failure, hanging from a thread.
Anticipating others' needs, dangling from the edge.
The thread is soon to snap, the weight too much to bear.
When you remove everyone else, I am
neither here
            nor there.

Costly Protection

I am something mythical
But not like a unicorn or fairy
Unfortunately for me,
I am something much more scary
Unpredictable, chaotic, painful and wild
A fortress of protections and guards
Surrounding my inner child
With spikes, and moats, and traps galore
And if you think you've unveiled them all?
Surprise, there's more!

Wrong Any Way

I don't know who I am
And I don't know how to be
It seems the rules of engagement
Don't apply to me
When I follow all the rules
There's still unspoken ones to follow
If I'm right, I'm still wrong
And it leaves me feeling hollow
Since I don't know who I am
I also don't know where I go
And if I don't fit in
Do I really want to know?

Despite It All

It's been a day,
It's been a year
And despite it all, I'm still here
Through pain and hurt,
Anxiety and fear
Despite it all, I'm still here
The past is plaguing,
Unknown future is near
And despite it all, I'm still here.

Misdiagnosed

I was so desperate to find answers
That I let labels become my identity,
Became a newfound serenity
I lost myself in ways I didn't even know I had been found yet
To have strayed, become delayed, so downplayed-
It was astounding
A noise that's so resounding, it's drowning out all the others
Like I'm becoming something other
I'm having a hard time because
I'm learning everything for the
First time
My lungs have adjusted to air outside this protective cocoon,
But I still can't see anything
I'm navigating this world without any signals
But I'm here
I'm Alive
I'm here
I'm alive
I'm here
I'm alive

As Soft as I Am Loud

I've been pushed back, pushed down, and pushed around
I've been told to swallow my emotions like I swallow these pills
Large, small, orange, white, take them at night "are you alright?"
I'd be better if my prognosis wasn't forever
If I could just get it together
Contain the pain within my brain
Living day to day, mundane, the same
But I cannot be muted, dampened nor subdued
I am an orchestra of emotions, powerful and loud
I'm proud of who I am, where I've come, where I'm yet to go
I am fireworks that light up the sky
Glitter crackling down to the ground below
I can be as soft as I am loud
Like the pale blue petals of forget-me-nots
Or the translucent rainbow refracted through the window

Borrowed Bars

I didn't build this prison
But now I'm the warden with the key
Why do I remain behind these bars
That I don't believe in?
I could've stepped through this cage,
I don't even need the key
Or, the key was not taking others' words as truths in the first place
Why do so many people lie?

Now To Be

I'm an out of the box thinker
Who was taught to color within the lines
I'm learning to unlearn what I have learned
and redefine what it is simply just to be
Decades have drowned in Shakespeare's ultimate question
I've thought too much about Not to Be
Now is my time To Be

Marshland

It rained in my soul today
It rained, it rained
It poured
My heart became so flooded
It pooled, it pooled
It moored
I then became so stagnant
No shot to shoot,
No score
I wallowed in my marshy home
Aloof, alone
No more

Flower Garden

Today I pushed up marigolds
because they overtook my garden
I tried to deal with all of them
Before the dirt could harden
I pulled some weeds
And watered what was left behind
If only I could treat myself
With patience just as kind

    Today I pushed up forget-me-nots
    Because they would not stop growing
    I worked late into the day
    Until all my garden lamps were glowing
    I wish I tried just as hard with maintenance on myself
    But oftentimes I bottle up emotions on the shelf

Today I pushed up lilac roots
To straighten out their beauty
I tried to hold in my tears
But the water works went through me
If only I could nourish
The garden with my pain
I'd have succulent bouquets so nice
But couldn't view myself the same

      Today I pushed up daisies
      Because I gave up on myself
      I'd taken care of those around me
      And ignored my cries for help
      Though I am no longer here
      I've got one more lesson for you
      Just remember that you need
      To tend to yourself too

Bravo

I said bravo to the sun,
When it was just doing its job.
It rose and fell, a pattern we know well-
Warming our days with a smile

I admired the waterfall's beauty,
When all it did was exist.
The water flowed down, a magnificent sound-
Mesmerizing us all the while

I minimize my accomplishments,
And criticize all that I do.
I survived more than most, trauma's own host-
Why do I put myself on trial?

Empty Hands, Heavy Heart

I carry too much on my shoulders
I carry too much in my heart
I give away the best parts of me
Then I'm left alone in the dark
I suffer for other people
In hopes to reduce their pain
But it's always a vicious cycle,
Sure to begin again
How do I share my heart
And still have some left for me?
At the end of the day,
if things don't change
I'm stuck with this misery.

Platitudes Needn't Apply

I do not believe "everything happens for a reason"
There was no reason for a grown man to shed his sin
And hide behind the disguise of piety
There was no reasoning with the torment of growing up as me
What didn't kill me left me wishing that it did
But I made myself stronger by healing through the
perplexing mess
I did the work to undo the damage that can't be undone
I forged new pathways and paved my way outside of the
confines of time
When life stacks the cards against you over and over
beginning at the ripe age of three
Sometimes your biggest saving grace is creativity
So, what has and hasn't happened
Will continue to be or not to be

The Journey I Didn't Choose

I am a fraction of myself,
Of who I'm meant to be.
The rest of me is locked in that closet
And he threw away the key.
I was forced on a journey
That my brain made me forget,
But that didn't stop the pain
From messing with my head.
Now I'm on a different journey,
One that sets me free.
I'm getting reacquainted
With my inner me.

The Postcard

I'm writing to let you know
I'm letting go-
I've held on for so long
And while that wasn't wrong,
It was causing me layers of pain
All for a man's sick sense of gain
I was stripped of a life
I'll never get to live
With fragmented memories
I'm left to sieve
It hurts to let go,
It hurts more to hold on
The past built me a shell,
But it's me that's been strong
Goodbye, adieu, adios, and so long

Beyond What Was Done

I am more than the pain that consumes me
At least, I want to be
I am more than what's been done to me
And yet I can't break free
I long to be free to be
I never got the chance to build my own identity
So, who can I be?
Why, I can be anything!
I used to be anywhere-
Out of my head, out of my body, out of the moment
And before I run out of time
I'd like to make a life that's mine
I remain kind despite the cruelty
And that's something that I'll keep
What other ingredients make up me?
I'm creative and thoughtful, compassionate too
I'm intelligent and perseverant-
If only child-me knew
I've been a victim, a warrior, a survivor
Now I want the chance to meet Laura,
Separate from the horror

I Am Not Back Then

I am not back then
But I remember where I've been
I cannot erase the damage
Of someone else's sin
And at the same time
It doesn't dictate where I'm going
Although I often yearn for
A future where my past isn't showing
As I tuck away those parts of me
I leave the night light on
I may not have been safe back then
But now there's nothing wrong
I take a look around
I breathe the fresh air in
I'm grateful for the present-
A reprieve from the grim
Now the future tries to tempt me
History does repeat itself
But I stopped avoiding the past
So I've learned my lessons well
If there ever was a cycle
It stops spinning with me
And this time back then
Remains history

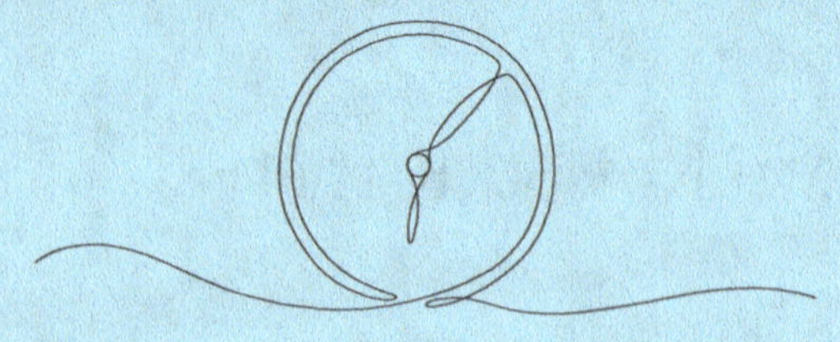

The Grief Compendium

An Ode

Everything tastes grey
Colors are faded too
Is this the new normal?
My life without you

I could've should've would've
And if there's one thing that is true
I cannot accept
My life without you

My love for you goes on
Even if you weren't able to
I will forever spend
My life remembering you

She's A Remarkable Angel, Honestly

Of the many painful times
That life has in store
Some of them affect just a few,
Others impact more
Grief, sorrow, anger, hurt
Amongst feelings that death brings
There is a silver lining,
A hope to which I cling
While loss touches all of us,
An inescapable thing
Shedding the heaviness of life,
An Angel grew her wings

I Am Here Right Now:
Special Preview

218

~~"Happy" Two Year~~ Anniversary
Happy Twenty Year Anniversary

Twenty years ago, today
I'm sorry that you felt that pain
Your skin should've never felt that blade,
At least never in that way.
The first cut, first prick of blood
Wish it hadn't felt so good
You did all the things you knew you could
Came at yourself with all the "shoulds"
People change and addictions fade
I can finally say that I'm okay
Yeah, you did it- today's the day!
Though it took a while, pushed through doubt
Got through the pain,
Finally figured it out
Part of me couldn't let go
And sure, I do have scars to show
They're from the battles that I faced alone
And yes, what you've faced is aghast
I no longer dwell in the wells of the past
I've reclaimed the 21st of December
I'll be thankful for you as long as I can remember
This is my past, a survivor

RE: I Am Not Back Then: Chapter "The Beginning"

Borrowed Bars (Reintegrated)

I didn't build this prison
But now I'm the warden with the key
Why do I remain behind these bars
That I don't believe in?
I could've stepped through this cage,
I don't even need the key
Or, the key was not taking others' words as truths
in the first place
Why do so many people lie?
I contemplate this point and come to the
conclusion:
I can only control my own actions.
So, I unlock the cage on my mind,
I am free,
I am me

RE: I Am Not Back Then: Chapter "The... End?"

Bravo (Reintegrated)

I said bravo to the sun,
When it was just doing its job.
It rose and fell, a pattern we know well-
Warming our days with a smile

I admired the waterfall's beauty,
When all it did was exist.
The water flowed down, a magnificent sound-
Mesmerizing us all the while

I minimized my accomplishments,
And criticized all that I did.
I survived more than most, once trauma's host-
I'm no longer putting myself on trial.

RE: I Am Not Back Then: Chapter
"The... End?"

Dancing Through the Nuance

Your dreams won't come true
If you simply just wish them
You need to put in the work
So they can come to fruition

My Best Possible Self

My best possible self is always growing,
It's connected, present and compassionate-
Even when my demons are showing
It's feeling the chaotic energy and not letting it control me
It's understanding and love-
in the absence of knowing
My best possible self leaves space for others and me
It doesn't abandon ship in the middle of open sea
it doesn't wade with sharks in the water
It doesn't send me out to the slaughter
It considers me in the face of all others
It doesn't hide me in shame under covers
My best possible self has been hidden for some time
But through self-compassion and self-love
I think she's finally mine

The Best Thing that Never Happened

The best thing that never happened
Almost happened several times
It's something I wanted more than anything
Until it was finally mine
And even though the want still comes and goes
Had I succeeded in those moments
I would never know
The best thing that never happened
Allowed me to stay
While new doors, windows, and cages
Opened each new day
It also taught me that
What we want we may not need,
It's why my happiest phrase is
"I did not succeed"

Let Someone Help You

United States
- 988 Suicide & Crisis Lifeline
  - Call or text 988 — 24/7, free, confidential support
- Crisis Text Line
  - Text HOME to 741741
- NAMI — National Alliance on Mental Illness
  - nami.org — Education, support, and referrals
- RAINN — National Sexual Assault Hotline
  - 800-656-HOPE (4673) | rainn.org
  - Text HOPE to 64673
- To Write Love on Her Arms — Support and hope for people struggling with depression, addiction, self-injury, and suicide
  - twloha.com/findhelp

Canada
- Talk Suicide Canada
  - 1-833-456-4566 | 988.ca
  - Call or text 988 — 24/7, free, confidential support

United Kingdom & Ireland
- Samaritans
  - 116 123 | samaritans.org

Australia
- Lifeline Australia
  - 13 11 14 | lifeline.org.au
- Blue Knot Foundation
  - blueknot.org.au — Complex trauma support

International
- Find a Helpline
  - findahelpline.com — Global crisis helpline directory (130+ countries)

If you are in immediate danger, please contact local emergency services.